Things She Never Expected

ALSO BY JAKETA A. MCCLURE

Rodeo

Things She Never Expected

Jaketa A. McClure

GIG

GIG Publishing

Benton, AR

Cover Design by Jaketa A. McClure

Author Photo taken by Mandy Holiman of Mandy Holiman Photography

Scripture quotations are taken from the *Holy Bible,* the King James Version of the Bible.

Printed in the United States of America

www.gigpublishing.com

ISBN: 978-0-692-19452-2

For all the single mothers, the married mothers, the widows, and the barren women, who thinks God has forgotten about you. He hasn't. He hears you. He sees you. He'll never leave you nor forsake you and neither will He leave you to try to figure out life on your own.

Love.

"...But where sin abounded, grace did much more abound..."

-Romans 5:20

Things She Never Expected

Chapter 1

She pinched him. Not too hard. It was just something she did to see if she could get a response out of him. Anything.

He really is a vegetable, she thought.

January 2nd. Three months in and he was still unconscious, but thanks to life support, he was still holding on. She sat on a green, recliner chair, next to his bedside, looking at the many tubes running from his mouth and arms. She quickly turned away. Looking towards the hospital windows, she stared out at the night sky. Sometimes, she couldn't bear to look at him.

Yet, she was there every day. Watching and waiting. Hoping, that today would be the day that her husband would wake up. And every day, just thinking about that tragic car accident, made her teary eyed. Just then, as she began to think the tears that were trying to force their way out of her eyes would succeed, there was a knock at the door.

She cleared her throat, "Come in."

It was Tina, one of her husband's registered nurses.

"You staying tonight, Mrs. Carmichael?"

Savannah nodded her head as she yawned and stretched out her 5'8 stature, turning her body here and there to work out all the kinks.

"You know," Tina started, as she walked over to her patient's bedside, "You *can* go home and get some rest."

She looked at Savannah and smiled, adding, in her thick Spanish accent, "He's in good hands."

Savannah smiled weakly. A tiresome sigh escaped from her mouth.

"I know. I just," she paused, finger combing her short, black hair. "I just want to be here when he wakes up, that's all."

Tina nodded, understanding completely. As she checked his vitals and fluids, she asked, "Any word on the investigation?"

The investigation. Just four days after the media displayed the deadly, five, car piled up, that her husband her been involved in, Savannah learned that the brake line on his car had been cut. As a result, a young, male, college student and an elderly woman died. Four, seriously injured, including, a five-year old girl. This turned that tragic accident, into a tragic homicide. Savannah tried her best not to be ungrateful because, even though, he husband was in a coma, he was alive. Still, she wanted all of him alive.

"No. Nothing yet."

"Have you eaten anything?"

"Not yet, but I will."

Even though, Savannah tried to sound as assuring as she could, she knew Tina didn't believe her. That was evident by the way she placed her hand on her hip and looked at her sideways. She shook her head, the way a mother would do a child when they were disappointed. Her fluffy, shoulder-length, black curls bounced here and there. Savannah knew, when Tina was on duty, she was going to receive all kinds of questions. Mainly, concerning herself, which she didn't mind at all.

She knew Tina worried about her and that her intentions were good. She knew, by Tina being in her sixties, with 5 kids and 12 grandkids, it was in her nature to be that motherly type of person. Most of all, Savannah knew that Tina had taken a liking to her over the time that she'd been there.

Savannah was grateful for Tina. Besides Julius, her husband's brother, she considered her to be the only person she could call a friend. And even with Julius, Savannah felt that she could only tell a man so much so, she was glad to have someone like Tina that she could confide in on a more emotional level.

Sure, there were people that Savannah associated with, but no one she'd call a friend. It seemed that anyone she once thought of as a friend had become more of an acquaintance over time. A lot of the people she associated with only knew her because of her husband and his social status. Savannah hardly considered the other wives and mistresses she met, at high-end parties, friends. They were just people who she'd mingle with and treat cordially because she saw that as being a supportive wife to her husband.

"Mrs. Carmichael, I'm going to bring you something to eat soon. You have to take care of yourself."

They both exchanged looks. Tina's tone of voice was so direct, yet, comforting and sincere. She flashed Savannah a slight smile, filled with concern and empathy. Savannah, smiled a weary smile, filled with understanding and exhaustion. Afterwards, Tina excused herself from the room.

If Tina was there, Savannah would always have something to eat and usually, because Tina was Mexican, she knew it'd be some exciting dish she'd prepared at home. Funny how she always had more than enough food to give to Savannah. She began to believe that she brought extra food purposely. Savannah looked at her husband.

"Lord, help me," she whispered.

Even though, many people knew what was going on with her husband, Tina was one of the very few people whom Savannah confided in. Being that her husband, Eugene Carmichael, was a well-known, Atlanta, Georgia, prosecuting attorney, the accident, as well as, the findings about the investigation, had been plastered all over the news and other forms of social media, every day since. Not to mention, one of the main motives behind the accident, that the reporters were focusing on, was that almost everyone assumed that Michael Espinoza had been the conspirator behind Eugene's failed brake situation.

Eight days prior to the accident, Eugene had an upcoming court date where crime boss, Michael Espinoza, was due to appear in court for his arraignment. According to Eugene, he had more than enough proof available to take the trail to court and he was certain Michael Espinoza would spend the rest of his life in prison. Michael Espinoza had been on law enforcement's radar for well over 15 years. He'd allegedly been involved in many drug trades and orchestrated dozens of murders, in and outside of the US. Although, the police knew some of this to be true, like many crime bosses, they never had enough evidence to indict him.

That was, until, Susan Galloway, a young woman who'd worked closely with those associated with Michael Espinoza, as a bookkeeper, came to the police. She'd accidentally overheard a conversation between Michael Espinoza and one of his associates, talking about a drug deal going wrong and having to permanently eliminate those involved. When she'd been found out, it was said that she didn't have to worry about her life, but she knew that was a lie. She came to the police for protection, along with, her bookkeeping notes, which recorded numerous amounts of illegal activity. The case was brought to Eugene and his associates because of their success with so many high-profile cases.

Eugene recorded her full testimony and even though, she was in protective custody, sadly, once she handed over her information to Eugene, she was killed. No one knew how, but just like anyone with a status, such as crime bosses have, it was believed that Michael Espinoza also had law enforcement on his payroll. After her death, Eugene wanted to keep the materials from Susan Galloway's testimony secret, therefore, he "put them away for safe keeping," until the trial. No one knew where Eugene had put the materials and being that he couldn't tell anyone, Michael Espinoza would soon be free, after being sentenced to only a minimum of six months for violation of probation.

Because of the accident, the arraignment had to be postponed. When that happened, reporters began to speculate that perhaps, Michael Espinoza was trying to buy some time, in order to get rid of anyone who could bring him to justice. That included Eugene. Which is why there were two, armed, police officers, stationed outside of Eugene's room, at all times. Just as they were at the home of Eugene and Savannah. No one was evidently sure if the Espinoza family was to blame for the accident, but it was understood that anyone who was following the story felt this way, including Savannah.

Because there was so much chaos going on around her, this was one of the main reasons why Savannah preferred being at the hospital. Although, she was still greeted by a mass of reporters whenever she arrived or departed, she didn't have to look out of her own window to see reporters hanging around her home all the time. Just the thought of it made her regret being opposed to living in a gated community when they bought their home. On the flip side, she was sort of thankful because she knew no one would try to harm her with reporters hanging around.

She tried her best not to worry, but it was hard. She constantly prayed to God for her and her husband, believing that he would protect them. Money wasn't an issue, thankfully. They had plenty of it. She just worried about her husband. She continuously prayed for God to take away her worrying, without taking away her husband. Selfish praying, she often called it. She'd worry about if he'd ever come out of his coma, and if so, when? She'd been confronted with the question of, "How long is too long to keep him on life support?" But, as long as they had the means to do so, she was going to keep him on it.

***

After much resistance, Savannah had finally succumbed to her mind and body telling her she needed a good night's rest. Savannah was pretty good at sticking to her exercise routine and on days like this, when it seemed like the stresses of things were starting to get to her, she'd go in her exercise room and work up a good sweat. But today, she just didn't feel like it.

She was now relaxing in her Jacuzzi tub, filled with warm water, bubbles, and Epsom Salt. She rolled her eyes as she thought about the herd of eager reporters, who'd been waiting for her when she got home. She was grateful that she could pull into the garage and close it behind her, without having to physically walk past any of them. No one had ever come into the garage but, she often wondered if one would be so bold to do so. Her mind replayed the questions she'd heard the reporters asking, from outside of her car window.

"Mrs. Carmichael, any word on the investigation? Mrs. Carmichael, has it been confirmed that someone from the Espinoza family was behind the accident? Mrs. Carmichael, do you fear for your life? Mrs. Carmichael, what are your thoughts about your husband's accident? Mrs. Carmichael, how long are you going to keep your husband on life support?"

She sighed. Then, she spoke aloud, exhaustively, "God, when will all of this end?"

She took a deep breath and caught a whiff of some kind of cleaner.

Pine Sole? Oh yeah, she thought. *It's Tuesday.*

Tuesday was cleaning day. With everything going on, it was so easy to lose track of days. It was even easier to forget that a four, women crew came on Tuesdays to clean their home, especially, being that Savannah hardly ever saw them, being that she was gone so much. But that didn't stop them from doing a good job and Savannah was grateful for that.

Just then, their Golden Retriever, Goldie, came into the bathroom. Savannah held out her hand and spoke as if she were talking to a little baby.

"Hey girl. Hey, my pretty little girl."

Goldie excitedly came over to where Savannah was. She rubbed and patted her saying, "Did you miss me? Did you miss mommy?"

Suddenly, the smile that Goldie had brought about began to disappear. Hearing the word mommy always made Savannah realize how lonely her home was. How she longed for a baby.

Eugene and Savannah met when she was a 21-year old college student, working at a lounge, as a waitress. She worked long hours to pay her way through college. Eugene, who was 26 at the time, had been out with some of his college buddies, celebrating his opportunity for an internship at a law firm. Unlike Savannah, Eugene came from a family who had plenty of money.

Eugene and his older brother, by 6 years, Julius, were born to their African-American parents, Stewart and Margaret Carmichael. Before Eugene and his brother were born, his parents would sell bar-b-que sandwiches in front of a welding company. Per permission from the manager, they'd post their stand there because it was located along a busy highway. They'd sell to the people who worked there and those passing by.

The best part of the sandwich was Stewart's homemade, bar-b-que sauce, which eventually, caught the attention of a restaurant owner and his pregnant wife. After returning home from a long trip, they'd been passing by the welding company, when the wife, who was "starving," suggested they get something to eat. The two of them were very impressed and the restaurant owner offered Stewart a job, working in his restaurant.

Over time, customers and people from all over started requesting more and more of Stewart's sauce. Eventually, it made its way onto the shelves of a major grocery store. Not long after, other stores wanted a piece of the action and they soon opened their own factory because the demand was so high.

By the time their parents died, Eugene had been practicing law for a while and was well-established enough, therefore, he gave Julius his blessings to fully take over the family business. Julius wouldn't agree to it. Sure enough, Julius handled pretty much everything involving the company, he still liked to keep Eugene close by to do a lot of the accounting and any of the legal matters they may have to attend to.

Savannah, on the other hand, was born to her African-American mother, Virginia Lewis. She never knew her father. Didn't know whether he was dead or alive and according to her mother, she didn't know either. Even though, they didn't have much, Savannah knew her mom worked hard to provide for her and she knew her mother loved her. She never had any siblings. At times, she wanted one, but seeing that it was hard enough for her to get, at least, some of the Christmas presents she wanted, she was just fine being the only child.

The night they met in the lounge, Eugene continuously kept flirting with her and asking her to go out on a date with him. After much persistence and his flattering comments about how his olive complexion and her mahogany skin tone would go great together, she finally gave in. Because she was trying to focus on her schooling and everything else she had going on, her plan was to go on only one date with him. After three months of dating, he proposed. Within a year, they married and moved into a cozy, little, three-bedroom house. This was a relief for Savannah because she'd been barely making it on her own.

They both eventually finished school. Savannah, with her music degree and Eugene's in law. Through much hard work, within 9 years, Eugene started his own law firm: **Carmichael & Associates**. It was sort of a bittersweet moment, being that, Eugene's dad had passed away only days after, and his mom followed six months later. Eugene and his associates were some of the most sought-after lawyers, handling some of the best profile cases across the states.

They had been married for a little over 18 years and they hadn't been able to have a baby yet. They'd tried many different fertility treatments, but nothing seemed to work. It had already been determined that it was Savannah who couldn't produce. "You're just not ovulating," a doctor once told her. "But there's always adoption," another doctor once said. "There's always a child who needs a home with loving parents." *I just want one of my own,* Savannah remembers thinking.

Doctors informed her that the likelihood of her conceiving was very slim and there could be many complications if she did conceive, at the age of 39. None of that mattered to Savannah. She was still believing that God would bless her with a baby one day. True enough, she loved Julius, Eugene's brother, but at times, she felt a little bit of jealousy arise, wondering how someone like him could have five kids by four different women and she couldn't even produce one. To her, something as such was an insult to people who longed for kids but couldn't produce any.

Savannah felt herself going into a slump. Her mind was starting to drift, and it was beginning to take her to a place where she didn't want to go. A place she'd been more than once. Depression. After so many years of trying to conceive, followed by a miscarriage, at one point, she fell into a deep state of depression. For a whole year she'd been someone totally different from who she really was. Eugene handled her depression better than she thought he would and with much medication and therapy, she was able to get back to her old self again.

Unfortunately, almost a year and a half ago, after another miscarriage, she fell back into that same dark place. This time, she could tell Eugene didn't handle it so well, although, he tried. She knew, him burying himself in his work was just a way to stay away from her. A way to stay away from a depressed woman, which made for a depressed house.

Once again, she had been prescribed the right "pain killers" for her condition. But God soon revealed to her that it was just that. Pain killers. Pain suppressors. They would kill the pain, suppress it for a while, but they never produced a permanent death. The pain, fear, and despair would only go away temporarily and then, it would spring back to life. Worse than before, it seemed.

After letting the enemy take her to the lowest point in her life, this last time, to the point of contemplating suicide, she finally realized this burden was far too heavy for her to carry. She refused to depend on medications as a way to narcotize her anxieties. Through much counseling from her pastor and spending time in the Word, she gave in and let God take control.

She was so happy she did. He took away all of her anxiety, her worry, her fear, her frustration, her guilt, and her shame. He replaced it with a peace which far exceeded all of her own understanding. It had only been a few months since she'd been back to her normal self and then, viola! The accident happened and everything else that came along with it. She knew it could be very easy for her to slip back into depression, but she refused to allow the devil to take her there again.

She got out of the tub and threw on her thick, cotton, olive robe. Then, she walked into her master bedroom, which housed a beautiful, cedar, entertainment center, along with a king-sized bed, a dresser, armoire, and two, night stands to match. She knelt in front of a Parisian style, storage chest, at the foot of her bed, bowed her head and prayed.

"Help me, Father, to be anxious for nothing. I am more than a conqueror. Greater is He that is in me than he that is in the world. I can do all things through Christ who strengthens me. I can get through this. With You."

She smiled.

"Peace, Father. Please, please, please give me the peace and the strength that I need to get through this. In Jesus name I pray. Amen."

Afterwards, she turned the radio on, located on her entertainment center. She tuned into one of her favorite Christian stations, turned the speakers up on the surround sound system, and let the sounds of music blast, as she praised and worshipped God.

Chapter 2

Savannah was feeling great. Much better than the days before. She'd gotten a good night's rest, got up bright and early to get in a good workout, and now, she was headed back to the hospital. Before she got there, she stopped by a flower boutique to get some Magnolias for Eugene's room.

When she arrived, she noticed that Tina wasn't on duty that day, which was okay. She just liked having her there. She went into the room and took out the old flowers in his medium-sized, ruby red vase, replacing them with the fresh ones. Then, she leaned over and kissed him on his forehead.

She looked at him, adoringly.

"I missed you," she said.

A slow smile spread across her face as she said, "I even missed you while I was sleeping."

She giggled a little.

I even missed you while I was sleeping.

That was a little saying they shared amongst each other. It started a number of years ago after Eugene had returned home from a 3-day trip with some business colleagues. After toying with each other about who missed who most, Eugene, feeling as though, there was no way she'd be able to top what he would say, said, "I even missed you while I was sleeping."

He was right. She couldn't top that one. She could only respond with a smile.

She grabbed a Kleenex tissue from his bedside table. She wiped the crust away that had built up in the corners of his eyes. Then, she studied his face.

"Hi handsome," she said, smiling.

She loved his olive complexion. It was so beautiful to her. She rubbed his thick, black eyebrows. Then, she let her finger gently trace the bridge of his perfect, pointed nose, letting it fall unto his full lips. She kissed him tenderly. She smiled.

"How are you, my love?"

She looked away, a little disappointed, at his inability to respond and picked at her fingernails.

"Could you at least wake up before the NBA Playoffs start," she asked.

She grabbed one of his toned legs, attached to his handsome, 5'10 build, and began stretching his limbs as she so faithfully did since he'd been there. Both of them were avid exercisers and she wanted to make sure she honored that for him in some kind of way.

"I mean," she said, with a smirk, "I don't know if the Cavs and the Warriors will go to the Playoffs again but, why not? It's happened the last three seasons."

She smiled and said, "Don't you want to see Cleveland beat Golden State? Or not?"

She chuckled a little, thinking about the fun they shared the previous year, when they wore rival jerseys and ate hot wings and junk food, as they watched the 2017 NBA Playoffs.

She began to get teary eyed.

"Nope," she said aloud, shaking her head, "I am not going to cry. Everything is going to be just fine. Peace, Father. Peace"

As she stood by his bedside, she closed her eyes and said a silent prayer. She was trying to practice instantly replacing her negative thoughts, with positive ones. Her new motto was: If I have time to think negatively, I have time to think positively.

Although, she was deep in thought, she was still able to hear the sound of someone opening the door to the room. She opened her eyes to see a young, petit, Caucasian girl, standing at the door. She was holding a baby carrier with a baby in it.

Savannah didn't want to seem uninviting so, she smiled a little and said, "Hello."

She figured the girl must have been lost. Still, she wondered how she was even able to get access to his room.

"Hey," the girl said, seeming both, unsure and uneasy.

"Can I help you with something?

"Umm."

The girl took a few steps into the room and placed the carrier on the floor. She spoke, hesitantly.

"Is this Eugene Carmichael's room?"

Well, she's certainly not lost, Savannah thought.

"Yes, it is," Savannah replied, now feeling unsure and uneasy herself. "Can I help you with something?"

"Uh, well, my name is Tiffany and umm," Tiffany scratched her head and then, she flipped her black, shoulder-length hair away from the right side of her face. The left side of her hair was fashionably shaved. Savannah could tell she was one of those young people who was going through the Gothic phase. Black clothes, black hair, black makeup, although, it was presentable, and a number of visible piercings and tattoos.

Looking towards the floor, Tiffany mumbled, "Man, I never thought I would have to deal with her."

Savannah wasn't able to make out what she'd said but now she was getting a little anxious. Still, she tried to remain calm because she didn't have the slightest idea what was going on and she didn't want to allow her mind to run amok with too many assumptions. The problem was, Tiffany's nervousness was making her nervous. She had to know what was going on.

"Tiffany, could you please tell me what's going on?"

Tiffany looked at Savannah. Then, to Eugene. Then, her eyes fell upon the baby.

Tiffany inhaled deeply and exhaled loudly, as if she were frustrated, saying, "Okay, look. It ain't no easy way to say this. Matter of fact, I never thought I would run into you, but seein' that your husband can't do nothin' right now, I guess I gotta tell you."

Savannah was afraid to speak. *Tell me what,* she thought.

Then, Tiffany let the words fall from her mouth all at once.

"This is Eugene's baby and he been payin' me every month to stay away. But since he been in this accident, he ain't been able to give me nothin'. So, I'm broke and I need some money."

Chapter 3

Savannah stood still. Motionless. She stared at Tiffany, who didn't seem to have a care in the world. In fact, she didn't care. She was only there because she was in need of more money. Savannah, on the other hand, was still trying to unscramble the words, "This-is-Eugene's-baby," even though, there was no other way to put them.

She shook her head and blinked a few times, wondering if she was dreaming or hallucinating. She realized she wasn't. She wished she was. She didn't know what to say. She didn't know how to respond.

With a hint of attitude in her voice, Tiffany said, "Hello?"

Savannah raised her finger as if saying, give me a minute. Her brain still hadn't processed what she'd just heard. She finally spoke, fumbling over her words.

"Um, okay."

She took a very deep breath, exhaling loudly, before continuing.

"Soooo, uh, you, you said that the ba-baby is Eu-Eu-Eugene's?"

Tiffany nodded, "Yeah," unfazed by the apparent disturbance this had caused Savannah.

"Well, um," Savannah paused, looking around, frantically searching her mind for questions and answers.

"H-how do you know for sure?"

Tiffany let out a somewhat, frustrated moan, "We already been through this. He took a DNA test. I got the papers in my purse. You wanna see 'em?"

Savannah shook her head and closed her eyes. *Lord, come on now*, she whined to herself. *What is this? Of all things. Do I really have to deal with this now?*

Even though, Tiffany didn't care how Savannah felt, she'd been hoping she would never have to run into her. Her main reason for even coming to the hospital was to see if Eugene was truly in a coma, as the news reporters were saying. She figured, by him being so popular and with everything going on in the news, there was a possibility that the doctors or his wife could have been telling people he was in a coma, for privacy or safety reasons. She stared at Savannah, who looked like she didn't know what to do. Tiffany was becoming impatient.

"Um, I gotta go. I got somebody waiting for me, so can you just give me my money and I'll get in touch with you another time."

Not only was Savannah trying to process what, where, how, when, and why, but she was really hoping that her husband wasn't a pedophile. She could tell the girl was young. Not only by her childish attitude, but by the way she carried herself, and her youthful look as well.

"How old are you," Savannah asked.

Tiffany slightly rolled her eyes and smacked her teeth.

"Legal," she replied.

Savannah looked at Eugene, concerned.

How on earth did you get mixed up with someone like this, Eugene?

"Um, could you please give me the money he owes me so I can go?"

With a raised eyebrow and a cocked head, Savannah said, "Excuse me?"

The only reason Savannah hadn't told her a thing or two was because she was still stunned at this new information, but she was really pushing it with the attitude.

"I tried to give him some time to wake up, but I done ran out of money, so I need to get it from you."

"Wait. So, how much money was he giving you every month?"

"Five thousand dollars for the last four months," she said without hesitation. "My baby is almost six months and for almost two months I haven't gotten anything from him."

Savannah's eyes widened, "F-five thousand?"

She couldn't believe he was actually paying this girl five thousand dollars a month. Just to keep her quiet.

Wow, she thought.

Savannah shook her head, not knowing if she was lying or telling the truth. About everything. She was also trying to quickly put a timeline together, in her mind, of when the baby was born and when Tiffany had become pregnant.

"Tiffany, I am not giving you five thousand dollars."

As Tiffany placed her hand on her hip and rolled her neck she said, "Well, that's what he was giving me and that's what I want."

Savannah, sick of this little girl's attitude, imitated her by placing her hand on her own hip and rolling her neck saying, "I'm sure that's what you were expecting, but guess what, I am not the one who's trying to hide you or the baby, therefore, I'm not giving you a dime."

Tiffany was taken back by Savannah's rebuttal.

"Lady give me the money that he owes me for this baby," she demanded.

"No. And I'm really disgusted," Savannah said, "That *this baby,* as you call it, is only a money baby to you. How dare you use that baby as your ticket to get money and spend it carelessly.

Tiffany snaps, "Lady, you don't know what I do with my money!"

Savannah snaps back, "I know that you've been getting $5,000 for the last four months and it looks like you have nothing to show for it, except for black makeup."

Tiffany scoffed, rolling her eyes and said, "Whatever. All I know is, I need some money now or I'm pretty sure with everything he already got goin' on, the news people outside are gonna have a good time after they find out he got a baby by somebody other than his wife."

Hold up, Savannah thought. *Is this little girl trying to blackmail me? Lord Jesus, help me.*

Although, that last statement did sting a little, in fact, a lot, Savannah was not about to let Tiffany see her so vulnerable.

"Let me let you know something right now," Savannah said. "If you're thinking you're going to blackmail me, you've got another thing coming because unlike my husband, I could care less what other people think. You see, I serve a God who is bigger than all this mess going on and I refuse, *re-fuse* to dig an even deeper hole than the one that's already been dug. So, you go right ahead and take your lil' sassy butt out there in front of those reporters and see who looks stupid."

The truth was, this was the last thing Savannah wanted the media to find out. She did care, tremendously, about everyone they knew finding out about this, but she was hoping the brave face she was putting on was enough to keep Tiffany's mouth shut.

She could see the uncertainty in Tiffany so, Savannah crossed her arms in front of her and added, "You telling the media about this is not going to get you anything."

Tiffany bit down on her bottom lip. She'd always believed that if she ever had to go to Eugene's wife personally, she'd have the upper hand and she would get what she wanted. She just knew that if his wife would not give her any money willingly, she would be able to blackmail her into giving it to her. Now, she felt defeated.

Tiffany spoke, softer this time.

"Look, lady, I could have showed up at your house, but I didn't want to do that. I just really need some money to take care of the baby."

"Have you been to my house," Savannah asked, quicker than she intended to.

For a split second, Tiffany thought about lying, just to further hurt Savannah, but she didn't want to further hurt her chances of getting any money from her.

"No," she answered, truthfully. "But just like anyone else could, I easily found out where *Eugene Carmichael* lives from the internet."

Savannah stared at her. Her face hardened, arms still folded.

Tiffany smacked her teeth, irritated.

"Come on now. I didn't make this baby by myself and I really need some pampers and milk and other things for the baby. Could you please help me?"

Savannah frowned a little, thinking about how she said 'please' but her tone and attitude gave off a completely different aura. Savannah started to tell her that it was not her problem. Yet and still, the compassionate side of her took over and she allowed her face to softened. Even though, she felt sorry for the baby more than anyone else involved in the situation, she knew the girl was right. She didn't make the baby by herself.

But why does it have to fall on me, she thought to herself.

Reluctantly, Savannah went through her purse, which sat on a chair, close to Eugene's bedside. She pulled out her billfold and took out all the money she had in it. She counted it and stretched out her hand saying, "Here. Four hundred and twenty-six dollars. That's all I have for you. Take it or leave."

Tiffany was hesitant at first. She knew she had leverage but, it didn't seem as if Savannah cared whether she spilled the beans or not. She was in no position to turn down any money so, she took it.

Savannah, expecting Tiffany to leave, watched her fish something out of her back pocket. She then, walked towards her as she unfolded the papers she held in her hands and tossed them on the bed.

"Those are the DNA results and her birth certificate. You can have those. I have copies."

Then, she left.

Savannah looked at the closed door for a few seconds. Then, she picked up the papers. She stared at the DNA results. 99.99%. Then, she looked at the birth certificate. Taylor Mignon Carmichael. Born, July 18, 2017.

She has his last name, she thought.

She turned her attention towards Eugene. Shortly after, the tears that she'd been holding in so well, let themselves free.

Chapter 4

"What! Four hundred and twenty-six dollars, Tiffany? What's wrong with you? Are you really that stupid?"

Jace, Tiffany's boyfriend, had been scolding her since she returned home from the hospital. She threw her hands up in defeat, flustered by his constant criticism. He shook the money in front of her face saying, "How we gone survive off this?"

As his 6-foot build stood intimidatingly in front of her 5-foot stature, she pleadingly explained that, "That's all she gave me."

"Naw," he said, shaking his head, "You gotta go get some more money."

"Jace, that's all she gave me. I even threatened to blackmail her. She didn't care about that so..."

"Oh, she care," he said, cutting her off. "She just know you too dumb to realize that so she played you."

"I-I," she stammered, "I took what she gave me. I figured anything was better than nothin'."

"Well, you gone have to figure somethin' out."

Jace tossed the money on a round, glass top, coffee table. He then grabbed a pack of cigarettes and plopped down on a tan, genuine leather sectional. He lit the cigarette and continued to scold her while he smoked.

"I ain't gone be able to pay my phone bill or my car note this month."

He shook his head.

"So stupid. You gotta find another old man to sucker into givin' you some money or go get another job at a strip club or somethin'. I don't know why you stopped anyway. You was makin' plenty of money."

Tiffany sat on one of the matching, red, leather stools, by the granite, bar counter top. She sat there, half-listening to her boyfriend of almost 6 months. Sure, he was smoking a cigarette now, but she knew he was high. The white, powdery substance on the tip of his dark brown nose was more than enough evidence to back up that claim. His many habits were the main reasons why they went through money so fast. She dared not mention that, though. The first and last time she did, it cost her a black eye.

Tiffany glanced around at the plush, one-bedroom penthouse, which cost them $1,500 a month. It was located in the residence of Buckhead in Atlanta, Georgia. When Tiffany first found out she was pregnant, she had an idea of who the child's father could be, but she wasn't sure. When the baby was finally born, she took one look at her and knew she had to be Eugene Carmichael's. In fact, she felt so sure that she gave her his last name.

Five days after the baby's birth, Tiffany tracked Eugene down, which wasn't hard, being that he was a public figure. She told him that he was the father and that she needed child support. He, on the other hand, let her know that he wasn't giving her anything until they took a DNA test. Her threats to go public with the information, as well as, to his wife, made for a speedy process. After confirming that he was, in fact, the father of her baby, that same day, they agreed that he'd pay her $5,000 a month, in exchange for her silence.

She'd met Jace a few months prior to her becoming pregnant. They weren't into anything serious. In fact, he'd been clear in letting her know that she was just a friend with benefits. When the baby was born on July 18, 2017, he only came to the hospital to make sure the baby was not his. A month later, when he found out she would be receiving a nice amount of money every month, he decided to stick around, making her believe he wanted to be there for her and be a daddy to the baby. Up until the accident, three months ago, Eugene had secretly been meeting up with her to give her cash, faithfully. Now, they had expended all of the money and Tiffany hadn't the slightest idea what to do next.

Tiffany had been so wrapped up in her thoughts, she hadn't heard the baby crying.

"Tiffany, shut her up, dang," Jace yelled.

Tiffany jumped up from the bar stool and headed towards the back room. She sat on the king-sized, pillow top bed and picked up her crying baby. She patted her on the back as she hugged her, shushing her to quiet her down. As the baby began to calm down, Tiffany felt her bottom, realizing she had a soaked diaper.

"Oh, you're wet," she softly said to herself.

She grabbed the pink baby bag that sat on the floor, at the foot of the bed. She looked through it and sighed out of frustration.

"Only four diapers."

She sat her baby on top of her legs.

"What am I going to do?"

She stared at her baby, hopelessly. Her innocent little baby, who was whimpering. Whimpering, waiting, and depending on someone to take care of her. Little did she know, the person who was responsible for her, didn't even know how to take care for herself. As Tiffany stared at her baby, that hard shell that she held up so well started to crack, and she began to weep.

Chapter 5

Savannah sat back in the burgundy, accent chair and sighed.

"You know, Pastor Larry, I hear you and I understand all of that, but you know what, right now, I'm having a really hard time living up to the way Jesus loves and forgives."

Pastor Larry, who sat across from Savannah in his office chair, nodded his head slowly.

"I apologize, Pastor. I don't mean to be so snappy, I just..."

Pastor Larry slightly shook his head, "No, Savannah, please" protesting in his husky voice. "Don't apologize. I mean, this, this is not something that one's emotions can so easily turn loose."

Normally, Savannah's days were spent at the hospital. If she weren't there, she'd be running errands or handling whatever business needed to be tended to. However, for the last two weeks, she barely left the house. Thoughts of what to do, how to do it, what went wrong, who to talk to, and if she should talk to anyone, amongst other things, constantly flooded her mind. She found herself in a serious slump. She couldn't even bring herself to talk to God as much as she used to or pray much at all. One thing was for sure, she was thankful for memories because it was her remembering that dark place she'd been, at more than one time in her life, that motivated her to get out of the house and seek some wise counsel.

Pastor Larry was the Senior Pastor at Yeshua Church. A church that she and Eugene had been attending for the last five years. Savannah and Pastor Larry had gotten to know each other pretty well over the years, with all the church picnics and gatherings that they'd had. She trusted him. Which is why she sat before him today.

"When did you last see him?"

"It's been about two weeks."

Pastor Larry nodded. It was quiet for a brief moment as Pastor Larry sought the Holy Spirit on what to say because he truly didn't know what to say. Neither did he want to say the wrong thing to further upset her.

He spoke, not too fast but not too slow. He wanted to be extra careful of the way he delivered the words to her. As if, wanting her to really hear and understand what he was saying.

"Savannah, I can't say that I understand what you are going through because I honestly don't, but I can say that I know this has to be very painful for you. I don't expect you, or should I say, I don't expect your emotions to forgive him or her right now. What I will say is, with everything we go through and with everything we're faced with, there is always test in it. A test of our patience, a test of our faithfulness, a test of our trust, even a test of our love. Tests show us our own heart. But, know this, when we are going through the fire, God is going through it with us."

Savannah was listening, but her mind wasn't all there. She knew that God was the answer but, her mind was too distracted to focus on even, Him.

"Savannah?"

She locked eyes with the built, brown complexioned, fatherly figure staring at her, with a raised eyebrow. She could tell that he knew she was only half listening.

"Yes, Pastor?"

"I can tell you're here but you're not really here."

Pastor Larry waited for Savannah to respond to his observation. She sighed. More from frustration than anything.

"I mean...I just..."

"Take you time," Pastor Larry said.

Savannah shook her head in disbelief and said, "It just seems like you're telling me that I'm just supposed to take this. Like, I'm just supposed to forgive them and keep on loving them like nothing ever happened. Like, I'm just supposed to accept all of this."

"Savannah."

Savannah locked eyes with Pastor Larry, wondering, *How in the world does he always remain so calm?*

"In no way am I telling you to just take this. And I know that you don't want to hear things about love conquering all and forgiveness, but what I am saying is, when you follow Jesus Christ, nothing is a coincidence. Nothing just happens."

"You have to give those cares to God. He cares for you, Savannah. Now, if we say we believe that He is an all-knowing God, then, we have to believe that he knew this was going to happen. Do you really think He's going to leave you to deal with it alone? Do you really think that he won't give you the wisdom to deal with it?"

She let her head fall, feeling like she'd disappointed two Fathers. God and her Pastor.

"No," she replied softly.

"Now," he said, sitting forward as he leaned on his chestnut, office desk, "You may not believe anything good can come out of this, but I believe, as Romans 8:28 says, He will make all things work together for good to them that love the Lord and are called according to His purpose, and Savannah, I believe that you are called, according to His purpose and, therefore, I do believe God will make something good come out of this."

Savannah sighed again, slowly shaking her head. She wasn't going to say it out loud but, she believed no good could come out of this situation. Nothing but, maybe, a divorce. Maybe it was true that she couldn't see past her emotions right now, but she didn't care. She was mad, and she wanted to remain mad. Yet and still, she knew she had to give her troubles to God. She just didn't know how to fully release them.

After more encouraging words and a prayer, Savannah gathered her things to leave. As she opened the office door to exit, Pastor Larry called to her.

"Savannah?"

She turned to him.

"Go see your husband."

She bit down on her bottom lip and nodded her head. Then, she proceeded out of the door.

Chapter 6

Savannah had never missed a day of coming to see her husband, in the three months he'd been there. From the subtle stares and double takes she was receiving from the hospital staff, as well as, the policemen on duty, she knew that they'd thought it strange that she hadn't been present in almost two weeks. She also knew that, from the quick once over one of the officers gave her, they weren't used to seeing her wearing a baseball cap with a black jogging suit and sneakers. Usually, adorned in some kind of skirt, dress, or slacks, with a nice blouse and some nice shoes, she'd found herself dressing more for comfort lately. Not caring so much about fixing herself up.

As Savannah neared Eugene's room, she spotted Tina coming out of another patient's room. She quickly ducked off into his room. She knew she couldn't hide from Tina for long. She'd already been ignoring her phone calls. She just hadn't felt like talking to anyone. Not about this.

Savannah slowly strolled around to Eugene's bedside. With each calculated step she took, she prepared herself for what she might say, even though, she knew he wouldn't respond. With her head held high and her arms folded, she let her eyes fall upon him.

A wave of mixed emotions swept over her. She felt hurt and betrayed by what he'd done. Embarrassed even, that her husband had had a baby with some young, white girl. She was sad because of the condition he was in. And angry. Angry because her love for him ran so deeply. She wanted to hit him. Hard.

In a slow, harsh tone, she said, "Wake up."

Her lips trembled as her eyes welled up with moisture. She quickly turned her back to him. She stared out of the window at nothing in particular.

"Eugene. You need to wake up so we can talk about this."

She thought that speaking her mind would be easier if she weren't looking at him, but as she tried to hold back the tears, a fresh wave of anger came over her. She turned to him and grabbed his shoulders.

"You need to wake up, Eugene," she demanded. "You need to wake up, so you can deal with this. This is your mistake. Not mines."

She shook him as tears fell from her eyes.

"Wake up! Wake up!"

Even though, she knew it wasn't his fault that he wasn't responding, it only made her even angrier that he couldn't. She backed away from him. She had to get out of there. She was far too upset to be around him. The last thing she wanted to do was hurt him more than he already was. At least, not while he was defenseless.

As she dashed for the door, it opened before she could get her hands on it. It was Tina. Savannah tried to avoid eye contact as Tina said, "Hey, the other nurses told me you were here. I've been trying to call…"

Tina could tell that something was wrong. Her voice was filled with concern as she asked, "Savannah, what's wrong?"

"Uh, nothing, Tina. I-I have to go."

Savannah hastily moved past her.

"I'll call you later," she yelled back to Tina as she hurried down the hallway.

***

On the drive home, Savannah was an emotional wreck.

"It wasn't time, Lord," she said aloud. "It was too soon to see him. It wasn't time."

Savannah was ready to get home just as much as the people around her were ready for her to get off the road. With tears clouding her eyes, she dashed in, out, and around others on the road. She knew the Lord had to be protecting her and everyone else on the road because if she'd gotten a ticket or in an accident, it would have been justifiable and her own fault. The only thing she wanted to do was get home and crawl into bed.

Yes, she thought. *I'll be fine once I get home.*

As soon as she pulled up to her home, she knew then that the thought had come far too soon. Although, the number of news reporters who'd been greeting her on a daily basis had depleted, she expected to see them hanging out in front of her house. And that's what she got. What she didn't expect to see, as she slowly pulled into her driveway, was Tiffany sitting on her front doorstep, along with the baby in a baby carrier, and a baby bag.

Savannah laughed out loud.

"Oh, you have got to be kidding me."

Her sarcasm didn't only come because of Tiffany's surprise visit, but it came in part because her garage door had gotten stuck a few days ago, like it had on a previous occasion. She could have easily had it fixed by now. Someone could have been out to her house the same day, but Savannah hadn't bothered to call anyone. It was her own fault for constantly putting it off, ever since she'd been going through her I-don't-feel-like-doing-anything phase. Therefore, she'd been having to go into her home through the front door.

She bit her bottom lip and shook her head as she sat idle in her car. Tiffany was watching the car, but Savannah knew she couldn't see past the tinted windows. She also knew she couldn't sit in the car forever. Honestly, part of her wanted to back right out of the driveway. But, as soon as she'd had that thought, she decided against it. Just the thought of her feeling as though some young girl was causing her to feel like she had to run away, gave her the boost of confidence she needed to get out of the car.

Savannah wiped her face with the backs of her hand. She put on a pair of black sunglasses that she kept in the car. It was still daylight and the last thing she wanted was for her eyes to give away the fact that she'd been crying. She gathered her things and opened the car door. As soon as she stepped out, the questions from the handful of reporters, waiting curbside, started pouring in all at once. One young guy had already made the mistake of thinking he could come on her lawn, just to ask her a question that she had no intention on answering. He learned really quick not to do that again.

Savannah walked in long strides, confidently, with her head held high. As she approached the doorsteps, Tiffany stood up. It took a lot for her to come to Savannah's house. She didn't know what to expect or how Savannah may respond. But she'd been pondering on whether she should come there for the last 5 days.

As Tiffany stood there, intimidated, waiting for some kind of greeting, she felt embarrassed when Savannah walked past her, without even the slightest glance at her or the baby. She watched her casually unlock the front door, walk in, and shut the door behind her. Immediately, she heard it lock from the inside.

Savannah leaned against the door with her back to it. She let out a deep breath like she'd been holding it in since she got out of the car. She could hear the reporters asking Tiffany who she was and what relation she had to the Carmichaels.

Savannah peeked out of her rose printed drapes, that hung from her living room windows. She couldn't stand those nosey reporters. She knew she had to do something about that, or they may go digging around for something and find more than she wanted them to. She could see that Tiffany still stood on the doorstep. She watched her bring her fist up to the door to knock, then, she let it fall back to her side. She could tell she seemed hesitant on what to do. Finally, she picked up the carrier and the baby bag.

"Why should I let her in," she whispered.

Although, Savannah spoke out loud to herself, she was really questioning what she already knew God was putting on her heart. As quickly as she asked the question, that still, small voice immediately replied, *Why not?*

Her mind was forming many reasons and excuses as to why she shouldn't or wouldn't let her in. All of which she knew wouldn't be a good enough or righteous enough reason for God. Savannah stared at Tiffany as she made her way down the driveway. Then, her eyes fell upon the baby carrier. With a raised eyebrow and pursed lips, Savannah slowly pulled away from the window, allowing the curtain to fall back into place.

"Because I don't want to," she sternly said and quickly, turned away from the window. She then stormed into the kitchen to seek the number of a serviceman for the garage door, feeling completely justified in her mind but far from it in her heart.

***

Tiffany sat Indian style, on a pallet she'd made, on the floor, in the middle of a near empty apartment. Almost all of the items in the apartment had been sold. Or stolen. She wasn't sure. She and Jace, but mainly, Jace, had decided a few days ago that they'd sell the things they had for money. That was on a Tuesday. Early that following Wednesday, she'd gone out with her baby to act as if she was looking for a way to make money. When she returned home, almost everything of any value was gone. That included Jace. She'd been calling and texting him, but he hadn't answered her or called her back and it was now Saturday.

Tiffany had Taylor laying on another pallet in the room while she smoked. She'd been smoking since she returned home from Savannah's house and she was already on her second pack. She'd felt so embarrassed after Savannah had gone in the house and closed the door behind her. Not a word. Not even an iota of eye contact. What could she expect, though? What should she expect? Truth was, she didn't know what to expect from the woman whose husband she'd had a baby with. But she needed help and that's why, after pondering on the thought, long and hard for many days, she'd decided to go there.

She sat on her pallet, surrounded by past due bills which were dressed in black and red letters. She had no money, no food for herself, and the baby was running low on baby formula. She'd used her last diaper that morning, and now, the baby was subject to wearing t-shirts as diapers. How foolish of her to spend her last few dollars on cigarettes.

Tiffany rocked subtly, with her knees pulled close to her chest. With every slow pull of her cigarette, she wondered what the chances were that she'd get the door slammed in her face a second time. She was all out of options. True, she could have easily stolen something. She could have even gone out to find some man to help her out. Of course, that was only after she'd helped them out first, but over the last few months, since she'd been receiving her hush-hush money, she'd gotten a taste of what it felt like to not have to do any of that. She didn't want to have to do that again.

Chapter 7

"I just want to be mad. Don't I have that right? Can't I be mad?"

Savannah had rushed over to the Courtyard Cemetery right after church. With her long, pleated, navy blue dress pulled over her knees, she sat on the plush, green grass, with her knees pulled close to her chest. Her back rested against her mother's tombstone.

"Mama, it's just not fair."

Tears fell from her eyes as she spoke to her best friend. Savannah's mother may have worked many jobs to pay the bills and keep food on the table, but she always found time for her daughter. Her mother's efforts to make time only made their relationship grow stronger as Savannah grew up. They remained close, up until her mother had passed away, 15 years earlier, from breast cancer.

Savannah always tried to find time to come visit her mother's grave site. She knew her mother loved flowers, so she'd bring her some fresh ones, like she did on any occasion when she was alive. She knew all that lay in the ground was her mother's flesh and bones, or whatever was left of it, but for some reason, she felt closer to her mother when she was able to come to the place where she knew she'd been buried.

"Of course, I love him still. I just don't know what to do. It's not like he can give any answers or any input. Why is that? I mean, am I just supposed deal with this all by myself?"

"I know God is with me, mama" she replied, answering what she knew would have been her mother's rebuttal to her comment of being all by herself.

"I just...but...this girl. This baby."

A short breath of frustration escaped from her mouth.

"I just don't know."

She let her head fall towards the earth for a moment. Then, she glanced back at the tombstone and asked, "Was I wrong not to let her in?"

She groaned. She felt ashamed because she already knew what her mother's answer would be.

"But why," she whined, "Why do I have to deal with this? This is not my mistake *or* my doing."

She shook her head and began to rant.

"I mean, come on, this just doesn't seem fair that I have to deal with something like this. I don't treat anybody wrong, I'm always helping people, I take time out to feed the less fortunate, and I am always giving thousands of dollars to different charities," she took a quick breath because she had to and then, continued, "I go to church every Sunday and help out as much as I can and I know I give more than enough in tithes and offerings and I..."

Savannah stopped cold in all of her venting. Almost, as if she were forced to. The revelation that had so quickly come over her, in all of her ranting and raving, made her feel so small. All she could hear was her mother quoting one of her favorite scriptures. The scripture she loved to say when it seemed like even a minuscule amount of pride was creeping into Savannah's heart or her own. It was almost like her mother was speaking to her from the grave. So sound. So clear.

She'd say, in her sweet but firm voice, "Baby, remember, Isaiah 64:6 says, "All our righteousnesses are as filthy rags."

Another one of her favorites also came to mind, found in Luke 14:11. She quoted it out loud, as each word she spoke, cut deep to the bone and marrow.

"Those who exalt themselves will be abased, and those who humble themselves, will be exalted."

She chucked a little and looked up saying, "What a way to humble me, huh?"

She got a little teary eyed as she thought of who she'd become. More than that, the type of Christian she'd become. The kind that had become so comfortable with their life, trusting more in their riches and status over God. Believing that, all she was doing secured her a spot in heaven.

With her head hung low, she whispered, "Forgive me, Father. I guess I," she shrugged, "I guess I had gotten so comfortable with my life and all that I had, I wasn't realizing what I was becoming. I forgot where I had come from and who brought me to the place where I am now."

She chuckled again saying, "I must sound so stupid talking about all that *I* have been doing."

She shook her head and said, "I'm so sorry. But why this, though, God? Why this? Of all things, why this?"

Tears welled up in her eyes again as she spoke. She shook her head saying, "It can be so hard to trust an invisible God. Especially, when you just don't know."

She sat quiet for a moment.

"But I trust You, Lord," she finally said. "I believe, but please, please help my unbelief, Lord."

Then, she asked something of the Father that she knew would be granted, which is why she hesitated at first.

"Give me another chance to make it right. Please?"

She sat for a few minutes longer. Thinking about what was, what is, and what might be. Before she got up to leave, she said, "Pray for me, mama."

***

Savannah sat in her car, in her driveway. She'd opened the now fixed, garage door, but she hadn't pulled in. She stared in front of her, at the back of Eugene's black, BMW 8 Series Coupe. She couldn't count how times, since finding out about Tiffany and the baby, she'd thought about ramming her black, BMW X5 into it. Yes, she was mad, but she wasn't about to give out unnecessary money.

She looked toward the front of her home. She wasn't in complete shock because she knew that there was a possibility that something like this might happen. Thanks to a very heartfelt, written letter to the Board of the Homeowners Association, they'd somehow banned the reporters from being able to come into the community so freely and loiter around her home. Therefore, she didn't have to deal with them. Still, she didn't expect *this* to happen so soon.

She looked up and, with a hint of sarcasm, she said, "Well, You don't waste any time do you?"

She chuckled and shook her head. She inhaled deeply and the long, hard suspiration which followed, was equivalent to the journey she knew she was about to face. She got out of her car and strolled up the walkway. Her black, short-sleeved blouse and black, silk skirt ruffled as the light breeze blew past her. Her black and white heels clapped against the concrete, with every step she took. She climbed the doorsteps, unlocked the front door, and held it open. Then, she looked at the hopeless, young woman. The young woman who was sitting on her doorstep, with a baby bag and a baby in a carrier and said, "Come in."

Chapter 8

Savannah squeezed her husband's hand as her eyes welled up with tears of joy.

She exclaimed, "Thank you, Lord," as nurse Tina gave her a high five saying, "There's no vengeance like the Lord's vengeance."

Minutes before, Tina had rushed into Eugene's room to turn on the TV. News reporters from everywhere were discussing the findings about that horrific accident, involving Defense Attorney, Eugene Carmichael and five others, leaving two dead. It had been confirmed, through a strenuous investigation and eye witness accounts, that crime boss, Michael Espinoza was the reason behind Eugene's failed brake line.

Of course, someone like Michael Espinoza didn't and wouldn't physically do the dirty work himself. And, of course, unless, one "cooperates with the police and turns over other names, dates, and information," it usually wasn't hard to find someone who would talk. Especially, after being threatened with life with no parole and possibly, the death penalty. His goons sang like a canary.

Although, it wasn't the evidence that Eugene had on him, but, with the injuries, endangerment of lives and mainly, the two fatalities from the accident, the courts had enough information on Michael Espinoza to put him away for many years. He was already 68 years old. Even with only 30 years, there was a slim possibility that he would he would live to see that long. Although, it was possible.

Savannah looked at Eugene and smiled.

"I'm happy for you baby."

"Hmph," Tina grunted, as she watched. "Now, all they have to do is put him under the jail."

"Amen," Savannah agreed.

Savannah's phone rang, and Tina excused herself from the room, to check on other patients. Savannah hadn't seen the number before and was with everything going on, especially, in the media, she was reluctant to answer it. On the other hand, she didn't want to miss any important calls. She answered, figuring she'd just hang up if it was a marketing call or something unimportant.

"Hello?"

"Um, hey, Mrs. Savannah."

"Hi," Savannah replied, unable to recognize the voice of the other person on the line who obviously knew her.

"Who's this?"

"This is Tiffany."

Savannah was completely caught off guard. She hadn't spoken to her in over two weeks, since the day she'd invited her into her home. She was wondering how Tiffany had gotten her number. It wasn't until Tiffany said, "I'm so glad I remembered I had your card because I really need a favor," that Savannah remembered she'd written her cell number down, on the back of one of her old, unused, business cards, that she used when she was giving piano lessons. She had given it to Tiffany as a way of her having the number, just in case she ever needed anything. Sadly, though, she was hoping she would never have to use it. She should have known better than that.

"Hey," Savannah said, a little unsure about what this favor she needed was.

"Hey, um, so, I...I really need a favor."

Savannah hesitated.

You already said that, she thought.

She wasn't trying to take credit for anything, but she'd already given her $500 and taken her shopping to get some things that she and baby needed. Savannah wasn't sure what she wanted, and she wanted to be obedient in helping her but, she didn't plan on being used by her either.

"What is it," Savannah asked.

Tiffany took a deep breath. She knew it would be a stretch asking Savannah to do something like this but, she didn't have anyone else.

"Well," she began, "I been goin' to the library to fill out applications and I been lookin' for a job but, I mean, it's kinda hard goin' to these interviews with a baby. So, I was just thinkin' that maybe you could watch Taylor for a while because I have a job interview today and I can't take her with me, but I don't have nobody to watch her and I can't afford a babysitter."

Tiffany took a pause from her rambling, hoping that Savannah would say something. When she didn't, she continued.

"I mean, I don't want these job people to see me with her cause then, they gone think I don't have a reliable babysitter, so they won't hire me. So, I was just wondrein' if you could watch her for me, please?

Savannah opened her mouth to speak but, she stopped herself because she wasn't prepared with an answer.

"Um, hold on for a minute, please."

She muted the phone and stared at it for a moment. She knew that she could help her out but, did she want to? She looked at Eugene, sleeping, so peacefully, it seemed. Then, she stared at Tiffany's number on the screen of the phone. She was almost overwhelmed with the thought of being alone with the baby. Her husband and Tiffany's baby. She shook her head. She couldn't do it. She didn't want to. She wasn't ready for that. She didn't know if she would ever be ready for that.

She quickly took the phone off mute and said, "Tiffany, I can watch her for you. I mean, I, um" she stammered, confused.

"Thank you, thank you so much, Mrs. Savannah. I just knew you were gonna say no but, I had to try because I *really* need this job so, so bad. Thank you so much."

What did she mean, *I can watch her for you?* She didn't mean to say that.

"I really, really need this job and I'm tryin' to do better but, it's so hard," Tiffany went on to say. "Thank you so much."

"Uh, yeah, sure" Savannah faltered, "I, I, I can watch her for you. Um, what time is your interview?"

Savannah spoke but, she was struggling to hold back tears and struggling even more to control how those held back tears tried to make her voice crack.

"Well, I have to be there at 1..."

Savannah looked at the time on her phone. That was an hour and a half from now.

"But," Tiffany continued, "It's gonna take almost 45 minutes to get there on the bus so, do you think you can come in a lil' while?"

Savannah nodded, still a little stunned from her unscripted agreement. Then, she quickly said, "Uh, yeah," after realizing she hadn't replied out loud yet.

"Are you still at the same place?"

"Oh, no. I'm at a motel not too far from where I used to live. I had to downsize," she giggled a little, obviously trying to make light of some of the noticeable tension travelling back and forth over the airways. Or, perhaps, she was only trying to make light of her current situation. Maybe it was just tension on Savannah's end.

After jotting down the name of the motel, Savannah let her know she'd be there and hung up the phone. She got up from the chair she'd sat in too many times to count and gathered her things. As she began to leave, she stopped at the foot of Eugene's bed and looked at him. She started to speak, but from fear of saying something she'd later have to ask for forgiveness for, she bit down hard on her bottom lip and walked away.

***

Although, Savannah was only trying to be obedient to the Lord's direction, those short two hours that Tiffany and her baby had spent inside of Savannah's home, the day she invited them in, were two of the longest, most awkward hours of her life.

She'd offered Tiffany something to eat, who gladly accepted it. She even offered a subtle smile, here and there, to try to ease some of the tension. Everything that Tiffany asked came as a surprise to Savannah. Not so much because they were outrageous questions but, simply because Savannah still couldn't believe that the young girl and her baby were in her home and she didn't know where to go with it.

Tiffany just seemed so comfortable. To Savannah, it was almost like, Tiffany didn't understand that, like her, she was supposed to be uncomfortable about the whole situation.

Uncomfortable and ashamed about everything that had transpired. But she didn't seem to be.

Every minute and every second was awkward, even when trying to make small talk. But, one of the most uncomfortable moments came when Tiffany asked Savannah if she could take a shower because the water in her apartment had been shut off.

What made it so awkward?

Well, for one, Savannah knew she would not have trusted her baby to be alone with a woman who she knew would probably have some ill will toward her and her child. But, either Tiffany didn't think of Savannah that way or she trusted people too much. So, Tiffany left the child in the living room area, in her car seat, with Savannah, and the baby kept staring at her. You know, that stare babies give you because they don't know that staring and not saying anything is impolite.

Savannah couldn't help but chuckle as she drove down the interstate, on the way to Tiffany's place. She chuckled because she thought back to how she'd said to the baby, "You know, it's not nice to stare." And how she made it a point to look forward, subtly looking out of the corner of her eye, to see if the baby was still staring at her. She was every time. She hadn't touched the baby or said a word. She didn't even look at the baby too much. She hadn't wanted to. Afraid that she'd see too much of Eugene in her.

Only seconds later, after pulling up in front of the one level, brick motel, dubbed with the name, The Atlanta Inn, Savannah noticed someone pull back the curtains in room number 5. The room Tiffany had given to Savannah.

"Lord, help me," Savannah said in a whisper. "Help me to not be anxious about anything. You know I don't want to do this but, give me strength, Lord and please help me to not treat this child bad."

She sat stiff, with eyes fixed on the tan door. When it opened, she saw the car seat first, then, Tiffany. Savannah was almost caught off guard by her hair. Streaks of hot pink and blue stained her styled, black hair. Savannah always admired people who did such things as that. To her, it was such a bold move. She had on red pajama pants and a black, dressy top. She figured she was still getting dressed. As she made her way to the car, Savannah swallowed hard. Then, she got out of the car.

"Thank you so much, again," Tiffany exclaimed. "I'm real glad you doin' this for me."

"Oh, it's no problem," Savannah said, as believable as she could.

Savannah went around to the passenger's side of the car and opened the back door for her. She patiently waited as Tiffany strapped Taylor in the car. Then, she turned to Savannah and said, "I shouldn't be too long but, I put more than enough stuff in there. I put extra clothes, formula and diapers."

Then, she extended the pink, baby bag to her saying, "I'll call you as soon as I'm finished."

Savannah nodded and said, "Okay," as she took the bag.

Tiffany smiled, sincerely and said, "I really preciate you doin' this for me."

Savannah nodded in acknowledgement. She could tell Tiffany was really appreciative.

"I'm glad I can help."

Chapter 9

His nose. His eyes. His lips. Even, his thick, black eyebrows. All of the traits that made up Eugene's face, also made up Taylor's face. She looked just like him.

How is that possible, Savannah thought. *I mean, I know how it's possible but, how...how is that possible?*

She studied Taylor's face as she held her. One thing she was happy about is that she was not a fussy baby. She was pretty calm. She also seemed very inquisitive. She stared at Savannah like she could read her mind. It intimidated her a little. She believed the child could sense some detachment. Some resentment.

For almost an hour, since she'd gotten home with the baby, she'd kept her strapped in, in her car seat, sitting on the living room floor. She hadn't touched her during that time or spoken to her and she'd hardly made any eye contact with the baby. Yes, there was an enormous amount of resentment present but, she'd agreed to do this, and her heart wasn't so hardened that she could ever neglect any helpless child or treat them poorly. Therefore, after a quick prayer, she fed her good, gave her a bath, and rocked her back and forth, until she fell asleep, all the while telling herself, that it would be over soon.

Tiffany was beyond excited when she called Savannah to let her know that she'd been offered the job she'd interviewed for, at Walmart. This was just two days after Savannah had kept Taylor. While she was happy for her, Savannah knew that Tiffany was going to ask her if she could watch her. This was definitely not something Savannah wanted to do. So, when she asked her if she could watch Taylor for two to three weeks until she received her first check, so that she'd be able to pay for a babysitter, Savannah politely said, "You know, there is still so much going on and I really don't have the time."

After she had gotten off of the phone with a disappointed, but, "grateful for everything" Tiffany, her conscience bothered her from that morning, up until the evening. That is, up until the point when she called Tiffany back to let her know she could watch Taylor.

She'd been having this constant argument within herself about why she couldn't, shouldn't, or just didn't want to do it.

"I shouldn't have to do this. I mean, I have other things to do," she said aloud to herself as she sat cross-legged on her bed.

Like what Savannah, she thought within herself.

"I mean, I have to look after Eugene and the house and..."

She sighed, shaking her head.

"I really don't have anything to do," she admitted. "At least, nothing too great to where I can't watch the child."

But what if I start giving piano lessons again? I mean, I can't do that with a baby around.

She chuckled.

"Savannah," she said, smacking her teeth, "Girl, stop making excuses."

"Ugh," she sighed in frustration. "God, I just want you to know that it's getting harder and harder to be a Christian."

Chapter 10

After almost three weeks of keeping Taylor, the hardness surrounding Savannah's heart had softened. To her surprise, she started to enjoy having Taylor around. Expect it, even. She found herself feeling a little disappointed when Tiffany would tell her that she didn't have to work, therefore, she didn't need her to watch Taylor. She even told her one day, "Well, you know, if you want to get out or something, I can watch her for you."

Savannah laughed about that. Who would have thought that she would eventually enjoy having the baby around, whom her husband had fathered with another woman? She enjoyed dressing her up in cute little outfits. She enjoyed reading to her and watching baby cartoons with her. She enjoyed sitting at the piano with her and guiding her little, baby fingers over the keys, making music.

She enjoyed the way Taylor found her so funny. The way her cute, baby giggle brought such joy to her. So much innocence. What she also enjoyed, was seeing Eugene in the baby. Although, she didn't understand her feelings toward him, she knew she loved him. And while, he wasn't dead, she felt like, having Taylor around, was something like, having him around.

Savannah hadn't told anyone about Tiffany or the baby, except for Pastor Larry, which is why she felt so comfortable inviting Tiffany to church with her, on this cool and bright, Sunday morning. But, as Tiffany, Taylor, and Savannah now stood in a middle row, singing and clapping along to the music from the choir, Savannah felt a little uneasy by the stares she was receiving.

Of course, no one knew anything about who Tiffany and Taylor were. Neither did they know from where they'd emerged. It's not like the stares were menacing in any way, but, she knew that some of the people in attendance were wondering who the girl and the baby were.

She glanced around the church, catching a glimpse of a familiar face looking at her. She smiled at the lady and the lady smiled back, then, they both turned their attention back towards the choir.

I must be crazy, doing as much as I am for Tiffany and the baby.

She glanced at Tiffany, who was enjoying the song selection, and Taylor, whom she held in her arms. A slight smile formed at the sight of them. Then, she chuckled to herself.

Savannah why would people just assume that, "Oh, that girl who's with Savannah is someone her husband had slept with and the baby is the result of it."

Savannah stopped reading into it so much. She knew how her mind would race if she let it, therefore, she just took it as people being their normal nosey selves. Wondering who's who. That was made evident after church service when one of the church ladies, who knew almost all the gossip in the church, came up to Savannah afterwards and said, "Hey, Sista Savannah. How you been?"

She was a little older than Savannah, by 10 years. Savannah vaguely remembered her name but, she'd seen and heard her a number of times, sharing the latest news about what was going on in someone else's life and "Only sharing because she's concerned and would like to pray for them."

Savannah smiled politely and said, "I'm fine. How are you?"

"Oh, I'm just fine, you know God is good" she replied, wearing a two-piece, olive green, skirt suit, with a big hat to match and an even bigger smile.

Her hungry eyes darted from Savannah to Tiffany to Taylor, multiple times. She finally said, sweetly, "Who's your friend?"

"Oh," Savannah said, as if she didn't already know that that question was burning her throat, wanting so badly to escape.

She pointed to them both saying, "This is Tiffany, and this is Taylor."

The slightly, wrinkled, brown skin on her face, tightened as she smiled and said, "Oh, ok. Are they friends of the family?"

Savannah opened her mouth to say something. Then, she decided against entertaining the woman.

Savannah smiled her sweet smile and said, "Um, excuse me, we really have to get going."

With that, Savannah motioned for Tiffany to follow her as she comfortably walked towards the exit.

Once they were in the parking lot, making their way to Savannah's car, Tiffany snickered.

Savannah looked at her.

"Are you laughing at that lady?"

Tiffany nodded, "Yes. I can tell she a mess. That was too fake."

Savannah chuckled, "You don't know the half of it. Anyway, Lord knows I don't want to start gossiping about her because that would take days. Let's go somewhere and eat a nice Sunday dinner. There's this place over on…"

"Savannah!"

Savannah turned to see Pastor Larry making his way over to them.

"Hey there," he said, offering a genuine smile.

"Hey Pastor Larry," Savannah said, with a smile.

She gestured towards Tiffany and Taylor, introducing them both. Tiffany waved, shyly.

"It's so nice to meet you both," Pastor Larry said. "I hope you come back to visit us."

"Thank you. We will," Tiffany replied, with a friendly smile.

"You guys can go get in the car," Savannah said to her, "I'll be there in a little while."

As they walked away, Savannah stared at them. She smiled a smile of warmth and admiration. When she turned back to address Pastor Larry, she saw that he was smiling at her.

"What," she asked.

"Well," he began, "I was wanting to introduce myself to them and see how you were but, from the way you just looked at them, it seems like you're coming along well."

She smiled and looked towards the ground, thinking about the journey and how she'd gotten to this point.

She sighed and said, "You know," she looked at Pastor Larry, "Sometimes I don't know how I even got to this point. I mean," She looked away, "I know it's God helping me, tremendously, along the way because I have really come to care for them but, sometimes..."

She paused, finding it hard to find the right words to say.

"Sometimes...with this situation...Eugene and her and the baby...I mean..."

"Savannah."

Pastor Larry placed a comforting hand on her shoulder.

She looked at him.

"You're a good woman. You're not crazy for doing what you're doing. You're just filled with the love of God."

Savannah looked down as her eyes began to water.

"Thank you, Pastor Larry. I really needed that. Thank you."

Chapter 11

As Savannah finally pulled up in front of Tiffany's room number, to take her to work and get Taylor, she parked next to a newer model, red, Chevrolet Camaro. She saw someone peek through the curtains in the room. Seconds later, the door opened, and Tiffany emerged with the baby and with her belongings, but she wasn't alone. Some tall, dark-skinned guy, wearing red jogger pants, and red and white sneakers, with no shirt on, followed behind her.

They exchanged words as he lit a cigarette and began smoking it. Afterwards, Tiffany handed him her cell phone and then, proceeded to the car. As Tiffany got the baby and herself situated, Savannah watched the guy. He'd gotten on the phone with someone, but he was still making eye contact with Savannah from time to time, even though, he tried to be as inconspicuous as possible about it.

Savannah, on the other hand, didn't care if he knew she was watching him. As much as she tried not to pass judgement on him, she couldn't help it. Thanks to Tiffany and their small talks about Jace, she knew too much about him. Too many negative things that hindered her mind from forming any positive thoughts about him.

When Tiffany was ready to go, Savannah began backing out of the lot. She tried her best not to act like she had the right to be all up in Tiffany's business, but she couldn't help asking, "Um, is that who I think it is?"

At first, Tiffany didn't say anything. Then, she said, "I don't know. Who do you think it is?"

Although, she didn't say it with attitude, Savannah could hear the sarcasm in Tiffany's voice.

"Umm," Savannah began, "Let's see. That guy you told me about. You know, the same one who took anything that was worth something from your place and left you and your baby high and dry. The one who was only using you for money. The dope fiend who hits on you whenever he feels like it. That guy."

Tiffany didn't respond. She simply looked out of the window, which let Savannah know she was right.

Frustrated, Savannah said, "Tiffany, really? Come on, now."

"You don't understand," Tiffany protested.

"Well, help me understand, Tiffany."

She didn't say anything. Savannah shook her head.

"You're right."

She threw her hands up and quickly replaced them on the steering wheel.

"I'll never understand going back to someone who would rather have cigarettes, drugs, and a flashy car to ride in, when there's no food or diapers in the house and the bills aren't even paid."

"It's gonna be different this time," Tiffany said, frustrated.

"Oh, is it? I bet he said that. *It's gone be different this time, baby,*" Savannah said, mockingly. "And I bet he was sooo sincere and persuasive when he said that, but his actions say he's still the same. You know how I know?"

She continued, not waiting for an answer from Tiffany, "Because he wouldn't have your phone right now and neither would I be taking you to work and watching Taylor, when he clearly can. And that's just a few reasons to name."

Tiffany started to speak, but Savannah cut in saying, "And please don't tell me he needs your phone and he can't do this and that because he's looking for a job because we both know that's some bull."

They were less than five minutes away from Tiffany's job and she couldn't wait to get out of the car.

"I wouldn't have even told you my business if I knew you was gone throw it back up in my face."

Savannah looked straight ahead as she drove. She took a deep breath, hating that she was letting her emotions get the best of her. She glanced over at Tiffany.

"Tiffany," she calmly said, "I promise I'm not trying to throw anything that you've told me in your face. I just...it's just," she sighed, "It's not just you anymore, Tiffany. You have a baby. A little girl who is being exposed to this guy who could care less about himself, let alone, about you and her. I just want you to realize that the stuff he did was not okay, and chances are he is still the same person."

Tiffany remained silent as they pulled up to her job. Savannah tried to contain herself, but as irritation began to reach the surface again, she started to mumble under her breath, but loud enough for Tiffany to hear it.

"Come to think about it, I'm glad he's not watching her. It's no telling what he might do to her. I bet he smokes around her and..."

Savannah heard the car door jolt open. She hadn't quite stopped at the curb yet, but before she knew it, Tiffany had hopped out of the car, slamming the door behind her. Savannah watched her storm off. She sighed heavily saying, "Good job, Savannah. Now you've gone and messed up her day.

She shook her head saying, "Lord, I'm sorry, I just don't want her to...I don't know. She's ruining her life. And just when things are starting to get better for her, now, this guy comes strolling back in and... I mean, why can't she see that..."

Savannah's thoughts were interrupted by the sound of a horn. The person behind her had obviously grown tired of her sitting idle for no apparent reason. Savannah quickly got out of the way of the driver and went to do some unnecessary shopping to take her mind off things.

***

After walking around some department stores, shopping, mostly for the house and Taylor, Savannah decided she'd go to the hospital. Over time, since

Taylor, she'd made some sporadic appearances but nothing like how she used. She swore that pigs would fly before she ever showed up at the hospital with Taylor, but here she found herself, sitting by the bedside of her sleeping husband, holding his baby.

After explaining everything that had occurred since Tiffany's first appearance, Tina looked at the baby that was sitting on Savannah's lap and said, "No wonder you've seemed so disturbed at times. I knew something was wrong when you missed almost two weeks of coming to see Mr. Carmichael."

Tina shook her head saying, "Never would I have guessed it was this."

Savannah nodded.

"His brother came to see him earlier today. He was asking me how you were. Said he couldn't get in touch with you. But I let him know you were okay."

"Thanks," Savannah said.

Julius had texted her just last night.

"Sis," he'd said, "You alright? I know a lot been goin' on with Gene, but you ain't gettin' depressed again are you?"

She couldn't help but laugh to herself. She didn't take offense to that because she knew how he was. So blunt yet, so caring. 'Sis,' had always been what he called her, even before she married his brother. They just seemed to like each other from the start, which made Eugene very happy, being that he cared a lot about what his older brother thought.

They had the kind of close, respectable relationship where they'd often talk to each other about the other's problems. So, Julius knew all about the depression and the miscarriages. Savannah knew how close Julius was to Eugene, therefore, she wondered if he knew about the cheating and the baby.

She'd been dodging his calls since she found out about Taylor. But she knew, that he knew, her behavior had changed. So, when he'd text to check on her, she just told him that she was alright and just needed to be alone. Anytime he had to drop anything off for Eugene, she instructed him to leave it in the mailbox.

"Well," Tina said as she got up, preparing to continue her rounds, "I know one thing, ain't no denying that that's his baby."

Chapter 12

The drive to Tiffany's had been quiet, at least, on Savannah's end. Tiffany had been making small talk about some of the rude customers she'd encountered that day. Even though, Savannah acknowledged she was listening by saying things from time to time like, "Ohh," and "Wow," her mind was still replaying what Tina had said.

Ain't no denying that that's his baby.

Ain't no denying it. She looked just like him. That's his baby. His baby. And Tiffany's baby. Not Savannah's. Although, Savannah knew this to be true, every now and then, that heartbreaking information seemed new to her again. Like, she had to process it all over again. And by having to process it all over again, fresh emotions came to her, all over again. Her thoughts were interrupted by Tiffany's voice. It was irritating her.

As she slowed to a stop at a red light, she looked at Tiffany who, continued to ramble on and on. Once again, to Savannah, she didn't seem to have a care in the world.

All of this I've been doing for her and her baby and not once, not once has she apologized to me.

Savannah became enraged. The tires screeched as she quickly pulled off the road into an empty lot.

Tiffany gripped the sides of her seat, confused and a bit scared as Savannah threw the car into park.

She yelled, "Do you have any idea what you've done, Tiffany?! Huh?! Do you know the pain that you've caused by having my husband's baby?! The pain that you've caused me?!"

A breath of disbelief and fear escaped Tiffany's mouth as Savannah stared at her with anger on her face and hurt in her eyes. Tiffany sat still. She was almost too afraid to speak.

"Hellooooo," Savannah yelled.

"I..." Tiffany began, still not knowing what to say.

"Say something!"

Tiffany dropped her head. She felt so small. She didn't know what to say. In fact, she still didn't know where all of that had come from.

An exasperated cry left Savannah's mouth as she stared straight ahead.

"You don't even care, do you," she asked, rhetorically. "You don't care that you could have ruined someone's marriage. Someone's life."

She looked at Tiffany who, still sat motionless, with her head hung low. Savannah scoffed and shook her head.

"I bet you get a kick out of going around sleeping with somebody's husband, don't you?

There's always some little girl like you, who thinks they can do what they want and flaunt their stuff around married men, not caring about the consequences or how it may affect everyone involved. As long as you're getting what you want, you're all good with it, right?"

Tiffany sat frozen, avoiding eye contact at all costs. She worried that whatever she said wouldn't be good enough for Savannah and if she did say anything, she feared it would only make her angrier. She could see Savannah's leg bouncing nervously. Or maybe, furiously.

"What do you have to say for yourself, Tiffany? I bet your parents would be sooo proud of you," she mockingly added.

Tiffany finally lifted her head to glance at Savannah. Then, she let it fall downward again. That last comment had hurt more than Savannah knew.

"Then again," Savannah added, "You probably got you scandalous ways from them. They probably really would be proud of you."

After a moment of silence that lasted too long for them both, Savannah said, "Get your baby and get out of my car."

Tiffany gasped softly. She looked at Savannah who, quickly put her foot on the brake and threw the gear shift into drive. She stared out of the window, away from Tiffany. Tiffany knew there was no protesting with her. Especially, after seeing how angry she was. Tiffany unbuckled her seat belt and opened the door. She moved in slow movements because she was still shocked, and she was secretly hoping Savannah would change her mind.

She carefully gathered the baby and her belongings. Once she was finished, she held onto the door and regretfully said, "Mrs. Savannah, you been so nice to me and I...I felt so bad about what I had did and I didn't know how to tell you that I was sorry for it, but I really am sorry for hurtin' you. And thank you, for helping me out like you did."

She shut the door and immediately, Savannah circled around Tiffany and sped out of the parking lot, disappearing into the distance.

***

"She has bus fare, she can catch the bus home."

Savannah said those words with more attitude than she'd intended to. As she sat parked in the lot of a convenient store, not far from where she'd left Tiffany and the baby, she thought back to how her mom had once popped her in the mouth, for saying something with a little too much attitude. She thought about how God probably would have done the same had He been right there in the flesh.

She hated having a conscience at times. She wished she could just drive home, forget what she'd said and done to Tiffany, and just go about her business as if nothing had ever happened. The problem was, one, she couldn't and wouldn't forget about the baby who'd emerged from her husband's act of infidelity, and two, the Holy Spirit was causing a stir of convictions within her soul and it was too much to ignore.

"Lord," she said, frustrated, "I don't know what to do. *I don't know what to do*. I've been trying to be nice to this girl but, why me, Lord? Why does this have to happen to me?"

Why not you?

"Because...I," she searched for reasons as to why something like this couldn't or shouldn't happen to her.

"I. Ugh! This is not supposed to happen to me. I was supposed to have a baby with *my* husband. I was supposed to have this miracle baby that no one ever thought would be possible."

She looked up and added, sheepishly, "And we were supposed to live happily ever after."

Tears began to stream down her face.

"I just don't understand. I don't understand. I mean, am I supposed to divorce my husband because that's what's going to happen. There is absolutely no way I'm going to stay with him after this."

She shook her head, trying to make sense of it all. Trying to make sense of God. She rested her forehead on the steering wheel. She was beginning to get hot, feeling as though she were about to hyperventilate. She blasted the air and let her window down a little. As she did, she was startled by a woman standing by her car door.

"Oh, I'm so sorry ma'am," the sweet, sounding, 70ish looking woman said.

"Th-that's okay," Savannah said, as she fumbled in her middle console for her sunglasses. She forced them on her face, trying to conceal any sighs of disorder.

She let the window down a tad bit more and said, "Can I help you with something?"

The fair skinned, petite woman stared at her for only a few seconds, but to Savannah, it seemed like a few minutes.

"Did you need something," Savannah asked hastily, her voice a bit shaky.

"Oh, well, yes," she began, "My daughter and I are just out and about, and I wanted to give you something."

The woman slid a Jehovah's Witness pamphlet to her.

Savannah sighed discreetly, thinking, *Ugh, a Jehovah's Witness. Why couldn't I be at home, so I wouldn't have to open the door?*

She took the pamphlet and quickly said, "Thank you."

As she began to let up the window, the lady said, "Uh, ma'am, could I share something with you, please?"

Savannah protested, "Well, I really have to be going so..."

"I know, I know. A lot of people frown when they see those "Jehovah's Witnesses" coming," she chuckled a little, "But, I just believe that the Lord has put this scripture on my heart to share with you. It's Isaiah 55:8 and it says, 'For my thoughts are not your thoughts, neither are your ways my ways.' That's what the Lord says to you dear. And even though, things may not go as we planned, always remember that the Lord is never wrong and nothing we do could ever take away the love that He has for us."

The lady smiled and said, "Blessings to you and yours, dear.

Then, she left to go catch up with someone else.

Savannah was stuck. She watched the woman, recognizing the passion she had for what she was doing. She realized God could use anyone He pleased. She sighed, feeling bad for wanting to dismiss the lady in the first place. Then, she put the car in drive and drove out of the parking, in the direction she'd just come from, hoping Tiffany would still be where she'd left them.

Chapter 13

Let's go get something to eat, was the only thing Savannah could think to say when she pulled up to Tiffany and the baby. She wanted to apologize, but there was more shame than pride present, as to why she didn't. Shame because she knew she was wrong. Sure, she was upset about it all, but she knew her mom would have told her she was too grown to be acting like she was.

As Savannah, Tiffany, and the baby sat in a booth at Olive Garden, she realized that this interruption in her life that she'd been trying to avoid, which had been forced on her, was inevitable.

Holy Spirit, she prayed inwardly, *just, please, teach me to deal with it accordingly because I don't know how to.*

No one had said anything. To each other, anyway. They'd only placed their drink orders and the waitress had just excused herself to go get them. The baby hadn't even said anything, and it never ceased to amazed Savannah just how quiet Taylor was. She just lay in the car seat, that sat next to Tiffany, on her side of the booth.

Searching for a way to break the ice, Savannah said, "She's such a good baby. Has she always been like that?"

Tiffany looked up from cleaning her fingernails, which had been her go to activity so that she wouldn't have to make eye contact or say anything. She looked as if the question had caught her off guard.

"Oh, yeah, she has. She hardly cried as a newborn unless she was hungry or wet or somethin'."

Savannah nodded, and Tiffany went back to her nails.

"Tif-"

"Here you go," the young waitress said, appearing out of nowhere.

She placed two sweet teas on the wooden, rectangular shaped table and asked, "Are you guys ready to order?"

Savannah looked at Tiffany for confirmation. She nodded her head.

"Yes, we are, thank you," Savannah answered with a smile.

Although, the waitress had unknowingly interrupted what Savannah was about to say, as well as, the guts she had mustered up to say it, she wasn't going to let that stop her. When the waitress departed, after taking their orders, she quickly spoke, not wanting any more time to pass between them.

"Tiffany?"

Tiffany looked up, acknowledging that Savannah had her full attention, even though, she wasn't sure what was going to proceed out of her mouth.

Savannah opened her mouth to speak, then, she shut it, exhaling softly. She wanted to take her time and speak. She wanted to make sure her words sounded as sincere as possible. She let her gaze fall upon the table as she spoke.

"You know," she cleared her throat, "There's a scripture that I really like. It's found in Ephesians 4:29 and it says. "Let no corrupt communication proceed out of your mouth, but that which is good, to the use of edifying, so that it may minister grace unto the hearers."

She looked up at Tiffany and said, "I say that to say, I'm so sorry. I said some things that definitely wouldn't uplift you and encourage you, but only tear you down and you don't need that. I'm even more sorry for my actions. You and the baby, Taylor, don't deserve that. I was just so," she sighed and rubbed her head.

"I've been so *mad* about *everything* and I've been struggling with this whole thing, but I was still trying to do what I know the Lord was telling me to do."

She shook her head saying, "You must think I'm so crazy."

She chuckled a little and Tiffany followed suit.

"But," she continued, "I'm so sorry. Please forgive me."

Tiffany smiled coyly.

"I, I'm sorry too, Mrs. Savannah. I, um," she paused, staring at the floor.

She felt the urge to share a little about her past, but because of how much she'd been burned by people she thought she could trust, she wasn't sure she wanted to.

Savannah could tell she was struggling with something. She asked, "What is it?"

Tiffany looked at her, then, she looked at the baby.

"I...I never had nobody do as much as you done for me. I know it don't seem like a lot, but I been on my own for a while. I ain't seen or talked to my parents for a long time. I don't even know if they alive."

She briefly made eye contact with Savannah, who was listening intently.

"My mom didn't want me. At least, that's what my dad said. She left when I was eight years old and I was with livin' with my dad. But when I was ten, I slipped up and told one of my friends that we had sex almost every night and then, the teachers found out and after that, I was in and out of group homes until I was 15."

She signed heavily, then, continued.

"I always ran away from the homes I was in cause I could tell that the people only cared about the money. They didn't show no love to me and hardly got anything for me, including food and then, there was men around who was just like my dad. I figured I could easily go get a job at a strip club, just like some of the other females I knew, and I could make just as much money as them."

She looked up and stated, factually, "And that's what I did. I made more money than I knew what to do with."

Savannah's heart ached for her as she listened. Tiffany's eyes wondered elsewhere as she shrugged, saying, "I done been pregnant before, a few times, but I would always get abortions or use the mornin' after pill. But this last time when I go pregnant, and I knew for sure it was Eugene's, after I found out who he was I told myself that this would be a good way to make some real good money."

She slowly made eye contact with Savannah and sorrowfully said, "I didn't see the wrong in tryin' to survive. I definitely didn't see the wrong in the way I was goin' about doin' it. That was all I knew. And then, you, you started doin' all this stuff for me and," she shook her head, letting it fall towards the floor, "And then," she paused, "I don't know. I, I could tell you was doin' it from your heart. Like, you really cared. I felt so bad. I didn't even know how to say I was sorry, even though, I really, really wanted to."

She slowly raised her head, looking Savannah in the eyes. Her voice cracked as she said, "I'm sorry. I'm so sorry, Mrs. Savannah."

She let her head fall towards the floor as she began to weep.

"I'm so sorry," she repeatedly said.

Savannah was moved by compassion as her own eyes welled up with tears.

"Aw sweetie, don't cry," Savannah said.

She moved over to Tiffany's side of the booth and sat on the edge of the seat. Tiffany moved over to make room for her. Not caring about the small number of curious people who sat close by, Savannah wrapped her arms around her, consoling her.

"It's okay, Tiffany. Everything is going to be alright. I forgive you. Okay?"

Tiffany nodded, acknowledging her apology.

"But," Savannah said, "Do you forgive me because I know I was acting like a bat out of hell combined with, Dr. Jekyll and Mr. Hyde, pulling off the road like that and screaming at you."

"Yeah, you were," Tiffany said as they both laughed.

"But, yes," Tiffany said, "I forgive you too."

"Come on. Let's got to the bathroom and wipe our faces and enjoy the rest of our day."

"Okay," Tiffany agreed.

Chapter 14

It had almost been two months since Savannah first began watching Taylor. She'd agreed to continue keeping Taylor, so that Tiffany wouldn't have to bother finding a babysitter. Tiffany didn't have a set schedule and being that she worked at a 24-hour Walmart, Savannah would have to watch her some mornings, evenings, and nights. Sometimes, Savannah would keep Taylor overnight if Tiffany got off too late.

Whether Savannah realized it or not, she was beginning to care about them both. It was as if her motherly instincts kicked in and she had inadvertently taken on the role as their caretaker. She found herself inviting them to go to church with her, every Sunday, when Tiffany wasn't working. She'd even invite them over to eat and chill out with her, on any given day.

One day, Savannah was studying Tiffany, while they prepared dinner. They'd just come home from church and Savannah told Tiffany she wanted them to stay over for a while, while she cooked dinner. Tiffany had confessed that she didn't know how to cook but, she could make some Kool-Aid.

Savannah had just taken a seat at the kitchen table, after she placed some lasagna in the oven to bake. She watched Tiffany as she prepared some strawberry or, "red" Kool-Aid, as she called it. She listened to her talk giddily about some of the things

Taylor had been doing like, trying to stand up and saying mama, amongst other things. Savannah liked these times. The times when Tiffany wasn't so guarded. The times when she would mention a small detail about her upbringing, good or bad.

Savannah paid close attention to Tiffany. She listened to how she spoke. Her movements. How she handled Taylor. She realized something. She was a child.

Yes, she was, by law, an adult, but her mind was still that of a young girl. Savannah didn't see that as a bad thing or as something that she should use against her to look down on her. She saw it as an unfortunate way of life for so many people. No direction. No proper upbringing. No role model or model of how a mother is supposed to be, how a woman is supposed to be, or how a family is supposed to be. She was just a part of a generational curse that plagued so many. Men and women. Boys and girls.

Maybe, I could be a role model to her. Maybe, I could be some of those things she needed. The things they needed, Savannah thought.

Tiffany aligned the garlic, cheese bread on an aluminum pan and placed it in the oven, as Savannah had instructed her to. Then, she turned her attention to Taylor, who sat satisfied, in her walker, with her juice cup and baby cereal.

"Hey Tay-Tay," Tiffany said, smiling sweetly.

Taylor bounced up and down, happily.

"Maybe you guys could stay here for a little while," Savannah blurted out.

Tiffany paused. Her smile faded. Slowly, she raised her head as her eyes met Savannah's. Tiffany was taken aback. Speechless, even. Savannah had recently entertained the idea before, but she'd never actually thought she would say it out loud.

"I mean," Savannah continued, "Maybe, just until you guys get on your feet."

Tiffany looked at Taylor. Even though, it had only been a few seconds, it had seemed longer since Tiffany said anything. It made Savannah nervous. Why? Perhaps, she cared about them more than she thought, and she was really hoping she'd accept her offer.

Without making eye contact with Savannah, Tiffany said, "But, what about Eugene?"

Savannah settled her eyes on a floral painting, hanging from the wall. She sighed. Eugene had been absent for such a long time. In a way, it made it easy to forget that he still played a factor in the decision making.

She'd briefly thought about how he might react to her decision for them to move in. She also thought about how it could take another three months for him to wake up. By that time, she figured Tiffany should have made progress and if not, she would put her in a place herself. What she didn't take into account was how uncomfortable he may feel or how uncomfortable Tiffany may feel.

She just felt so much compassion for them. She knew Tiffany was struggling and she hated the two of them being cooped up, in a motel room, with that...boy...who didn't mean either of them any good.

Savannah cleared her throat, saying, "He's not here right now so, we could just cross that bridge when we get to it."

Tiffany sighed. She was floored at how open Savannah was being. She was so beyond grateful for it. Sure enough, Eugene was asleep now but if and when he woke up, she didn't want to be there. She'd grown to respect Savannah so much, as well as, herself and she knew she'd be beyond uncomfortable in the same house as the two of them.

She liked Savannah, but she hated herself for doing what she did, and she wasn't sure if she wanted to make that move just yet. They'd been spending so much time together and Tiffany constantly had reminders of how she'd messed up Savannah's marriage. It was already hard enough to forgive herself, now that she was becoming this new person in Jesus Christ, so constantly being in the same house with the selfless woman she'd betrayed would only make her feel worse about herself. And, even though, Savannah had invited them to stay, she didn't want to be an even bigger burden than she already was.

"You know, Mrs. Savannah, I really preciate everything you been doin' for us and inviting us to live here is so great, but I don't know if I'm really ready for that."

Savannah nodded, "I understand," she sincerely said.

"I just want you to know that my door is always open and I'm here for you guys. With whatever you need. Okay?"

Tiffany blinked back the tears that were attempting to form in her eyes and softly said, "Okay."

Afterwards, neither of them mentioned it again. They enjoyed their dinner and the apple pie that followed, while occasionally, talking about Taylor, things going on at Tiffany's job, and almost any other subject that arose.

***

Later that evening, after Savannah dropped Tiffany off, Tiffany was greeted by a cloud of smoke and loud music, as she opened the door to the motel room. Now, she was even more grateful that Savannah was keeping Taylor overnight, since she had to go in to work late. Jace sat around with his friends, smoking and drinking, while listening to music and playing games.

"There she go," Jace said, with a smirk on his face.

Tiffany briefly looked around, unsure of what to do next. She quickly decided to go to the bathroom. As she walked by, Jace extended the bottle of beer that he was drinking to her.

"Here," he said.

She glanced at him, saying, "Oh, naw, I'm good. Thanks."

She continued towards the bathroom. She didn't have a reason to go in there, she just didn't feel like being around all that smoke and loud music. And, although, the bathroom wasn't too far from it all, she believed she'd still be able to find some kind of solace in there. Behind a closed door.

As she entered the bathroom, she heard Jace say to his friends, "Look at her. She been goin' to church and now she think she a good girl."

He and his friends chuckled.

"You think you a good girl now, huh," he yelled, as she closed the bathroom door and locked it.

Tiffany plopped down on top of the toilet lid. She rubbed her temples as Jace yelled other things she could hardly make out. She sighed heavily.

"Why is he always trying to start somethin' with me," she said in a whisper.

"Especially, after church?"

She looked up, as if talking to God and said, "Why? I always thought things were supposed to get better when people followed You. I don't know what to..."

She was cut off by a loud banging on the door.

"Yeah," she yelled, startled.

"Who you yellin' at," Jace said, angrily, "And what you doin' in there? You don't hear me talking to you? Open the door!"

Before she could fully open the door, Jace was forcing his way in.

"What you doin' in here," he demanded.

"Nothin'. Why you so mad?"

"You probably sittin' in here on the phone, textin' whatever dude you been goin' to see."

Tiffany looked at him and frowned.

"Oh, my goodness," she said, irritated, "Are you for real?"

"What you mean, *am I for real*," he said. "You ain't been here. You claim you been goin' to church and workin' and over this old lady house..."

Tiffany cut in, "That is what I been doin'."

"Whatever," he said. "Let me see your phone."

Tiffany smacked her teeth saying, "Jace, leave me alone. I really don't feel like this today."

"Oh, you don't want me to see yo' phone cause you got somethin' to hide, right?"

"Ain't nobody hidin' nothin' from you," she said, angrily. "And I know you ain't talkin' with all the stuff you be doin'."

"Oh, so you sayin' you are doin' somethin', right? Where your phone at?"

He snatched up her purse from off the floor and started digging through it, tossing things here and there.

"Give me my stuff," she yelled, as she tried to snatch her purse away from him.

"Ain't nobody doin' nothin' to you," she added.

He lifted his fist as if he was going to hit her and said, "Let it go."

She stared at him for a moment. She could see the drunkenness in his yellowish-red eyes, smell the alcohol and smoke on him, and she definitely knew what that small, white stain on his nose was. Although, the way he was acting was nothing new, at that moment, he looked so much more different to her than any other time. So much more...evil. She let go of her purse. She didn't want to deal with trying to fight with him right now. To be honest, she was getting tired of him all together.

She pushed past him, not too forcibly, but just enough to get around him. She didn't want to be there anymore. It didn't matter that her shift didn't start for another four hours, she decided she was going to go ahead and get ready for work, so she could leave. She hastily walked over to a tall, brown, four drawer dresser located on the side of one of the two, queen sized beds. Jace followed behind her. As she began to dig through the dresser, Jace demanded, "What you doin' now?"

Without looking at him, she calmly, but firmly replied, "I'm bout to get ready for work."

"Oh, I thought you didn't have to go to work until later tonight? See, that's the stuff I be talkin' bout. You always lyin'. You ain't goin' nowhere," he said, as he pushed the dresser drawer closed, closing it on her hand.

"Ow," she yelled, pushing him, "What you do that for?"

"Shut up," he said as he smacked her across the face, hard.

She fell onto the bed, holding the side of her face.

"Aye, I'll catch up with y'all later," he said to his friends, who were going along as if nothing was happening.

They'd seen him act in such a way plenty of times, so they thought nothing of it.

"Okay," they said, as they gathered their things and left.

As they were leaving, Tiffany quickly gathered her things and ran into the bathroom, locking the door behind her. Jace pounded on the door.

"Open this door!"

She didn't respond and neither she didn't open the door. She only coward in the corner, away from the door.

"Tiffany, open this door!"

Seconds later, Tiffany screamed as he kicked the door in. She could only cry and beg him to stop as he yelled all sorts of toxic words toward her, while beating her like he never had before. When he had exhausted himself, he returned to his video games, his drugs, and his music, as if nothing had happened.

Chapter 15

"Tiffany," Savannah exclaimed.

Savannah clutched at her olive robe as she stood there startled, confused, and fearful from whatever had happened.

She gently pulled a battered Tiffany, who stood on her doorstep, into her home. It was only after nine that same evening that she'd just dropped Tiffany off at the motel, but it was obvious to Savannah that something had gone terribly wrong between that time and now.

"Oh my, Tiffany," Savannah said, her voice filled with concern.

"Come, sit down."

She led her to the sofa in the living room and said, "Don't move, I'll be right back."

She rushed to a storage closet and gathered some of first aid supplies. Then, she went to retrieve a face towel and wet it with warm water.

When she returned, she began to doctor on Tiffany's face. She shook her head as she gently dabbed the warm towel over the black and blue bruises, clearing away the blood, which seeped through some of the cuts on her face. Then, she carefully applied some antiseptics and creams with gauze and cotton balls. All the while, Tiffany struggled to avoid making eye contact with Savannah.

Savannah knew that there was only one person who was responsible for what had been done to her. She didn't have to say it and neither did Tiffany.

"You need to report him to the police," Savannah said, as she began to angrily, gather up the blood covered cotton balls and gauze.

Tiffany shook her head and said, "He really didn't mean it, it, it's just with the drugs and all...

"Don't you dare," Savannah yelled, unintentionally.

Although, she tried to calm her emotions, it was obvious she was upset. She firmly said, "Don't you *dare* make excuses for him, Tiffany."

She noticed she was pointing her finger at Tiffany, like she was a child. Her child. She let her hand fall by her side.

Savannah tried speaking in a softer tone, with more logic.

"Are you really okay with this guy beating on you like this? Have you seen your face? I mean, really? And Taylor. Is this what you want for her? Because whether you believe so or not, she *will* be affected by what she is exposed to."

Tiffany didn't respond. She kept her face lowered, looking and feeling ashamed. Savannah shook her head and tossed the mess in a wastebasket. Afterwards, she finished gathering the first aid supplies and put them back in the storage closet. Once she returned, she found Tiffany crying.

Savannah watched the damsel weep. It was so hard not to have pity for her. She wondered why Tiffany couldn't see the wrong in this. Why any person couldn't see the wrong in many things. A scripture came to her. The words Jesus said, as He hung on the cross.

"Father, forgive them; for they know not what they do." Luke 23:34

Savannah was moved with compassion for the young lady. It's hard to see straight when your eyes and mind have not been enlightened. It's hard to know what's right, what makes sense, when you don't know the One who died for you. Tiffany was so disappointed in herself. She was also disappointed because she knew that Savannah was disappointed in her.

Through sniffled cries, Tiffany softly said, "I'm sorry I'm such a disappointment. To everyone. I'm such a bad mother."

"Oh, Tiffany," Savannah said as she sat close to her on the sofa.

She placed her arm around her and said, "Tiffany."

Savannah sighed heavily, pausing to gather her thoughts.

"Baby, you are not a disappointment. Do you hear me?"

Tiffany nodded.

Savannah looked at her through sincere eyes and said, "You just don't know. You are only a product of your own environment. I mean, how can you know if you weren't nurtured the right way?"

Savannah grabbed a Kleenex and gently wiped Tiffany's tears.

"Don't cry sweetie. Taylor is going to be just fine. Especially, if *I* have anything to do with it."

Tiffany looked at Savannah, sniffling, while trying to gain control of herself. Savannah smiled and so did she. Tiffany returned her gaze to the earth and, after a few seconds of silence, said, "I don't wanna go back."

"And you don't have to," Savannah said.

Chapter 16

"I love it," Tiffany exclaimed.

As both she and Savannah took a step back to take in the scenery, Tiffany stared in awe at how nice the room, Savannah and she decorated, had turned out. It had only been a few days since Tiffany had shown up to Savannah's, badly beaten. She had taken a few days off from work, but Savannah convinced her to take two weeks, so her bruises could fully heal.

Savannah had turned, one of the three, downstairs guestrooms into what could be called a now, nicely, decorated, permanent room. There was already a nice, queen-sized bed in the room, so early that morning, they'd gone to do some shopping to spruce it up a bit. They'd gotten a nice, cherry wood crib for Taylor, which could be converted into a toddler bed, along with a few things to go with it like, quilts, pillows, and stuffed animals.

They also got things like throw rugs, some nice wall décor, and other decorative things to add color and personality to the room. Savannah had even let Tiffany pick out a theme for the bathroom in the bedroom. Of course, this was all done at Savannah's expense, who was more than happy to do it. She would have bought more items had it not been for Tiffany constantly letting her know that she'd done more than enough, and she didn't need anything else.

For some odd reason, decorating the room with Tiffany was so exciting to Savannah. Yes, she loved to decorate, but what she looked forward to most, was having people in the house. Them, specifically. She didn't know how or when it happened, but she had come to realize that she cared about them a lot.

Perhaps, it was the night that Tiffany had shown up to her house all beaten up. Savannah realized she was so mad that she wanted to go beat him up the way he'd done Tiffany. Whenever or however it happened, she cared deeply for them and she didn't want anything to harm them. She believed them living there, with her, was the best thing for them.

***

"Tiffany, why don't you just got to school for something," Savannah said, as she drained some pasta.

It was around 7 that evening, only about four hours since they'd finished decorating Tiffany and Taylor's room. Taylor had fallen asleep and Tiffany sat at the kitchen table, making small talk with Savannah, as she prepared dinner.

"I mean," she continued, "You're here and I'm not going to charge you any rent because I want you to get on your feet and hey, you already have a babysitter. You should just go to school. You could even get a trade in something, that way, you don't have to be in school for a long time. You could go to a school where you can get your GED and your degree. I mean," Savannah continued, "If you ask me, I think you should go to school for hair because you're always doing something so nice to yours and adding some kind of color and different style to it. Lord knows you are a lot bolder than I am," Savannah chuckled as she glanced back at Tiffany.

She stopped once she saw the look on Tiffany's face. It was one of sadness. She looked as if she were getting teary-eyed.

"What's wrong," Savannah asked, concerned.

"I just, um," Tiffany began. "Why you bein' so nice to me."

She shook her head, feeling sorry for herself, saying, "I don't deserve this. All of this stuff you've been doin' for me and Taylor. I don't deserve it."

Savannah sat the drainer down in the sink and turned towards Tiffany. She wiped her wet hands on the black apron she wore and leaned back against the counter. She shook her head, searching for the words to say. She honestly didn't know why she was going above and beyond for them.

"Tiffany," she started, slightly shrugging her shoulders, "I honestly don't know why I'm doing the things I'm doing. I mean, all I can come to believe is that it's God. Sure, I should be treating you both like dirt, you know? Or perhaps, I should say, I *could* be treating you both like dirt. Regardless of what happened, I don't have the right to treat you two like anything other than a human being. I believe most people in my situation probably would, but for some reason, my heart won't let me."

"But," Tiffany said, "It's just so much."

She looked at Savannah and said, "You've been so nice to me and it's like, it's like, I, I don't know how to take it. Does that make sense?"

Savannah nodded.

"That makes perfect sense."

She made her way over to one of the chairs sitting around the kitchen table.

"Which further lets me know that God is working all of this out for our good. It also lets me know just how strong God's grace and love is."

She pulled out a chair and sat down. She then, placed her hand over Tiffany's and said, "I don't want you to think that it's a burden on me. You and Taylor. It's not. Okay?"

Tiffany nodded.

"I mean," Savannah said as she got up and headed back to the sink, "It might be a little selfish of me but I'm actually enjoying this time. You guys being here. It helps me not feel so lonely and keeps my mind on other things.

She turned to her saying, "Just see this as one of the many gifts God is giving you. And take it, thanking Him in the process. Okay?"

Tiffany sighed a breath of relief and smiled a little saying, "Okay."

"Now," Savannah said as she poured her bow tie pasta in a big glass bowl, "Back to this going to school for hair thing."

Chapter 17

"Hey sis. I hadn't talk to you in a while. Just wonderin' how you been?"

Savannah sat comfortably on the oversized sofa in the den, watching cartoons with Taylor, who sat comfortably next to her. When her phone had first rang, and she saw that it was Julius, she started not to answer it. At this moment, though, she felt the need to answer the phone.

Why hide, she thought. *From fear of what others would think? It's not me who did this.*

Still, even with the reality of that, part of her deeply cared about how others portrayed their seemingly, happy marriage to be but, with Julius, she figured, she didn't have to hide anything from him. He's her husband's brother and he seemed to be just as much her brother as he was Eugene's. She decided she'd tell him what was going on.

But first, she thought, *I'll invite him over to see the baby, just to see if he already knows about her.*

She prayed to God he didn't know because she knew that would surely put a damper on their relationship. Brother or no brother.

"Hey Julius," she replied, with a smile. "I've been alright, honestly. There have just been some things going on that..." she paused.

Then, she said, "You know what, um, are you busy right now?"

"No. I mean, I'm at the office but, I can leave for a lil while."

She smirked as she listened to him, thinking about how she and Eugene would often make fun of his slow, southern twang.

"Good. Can you come over? I need to show you something."

Someone, she thought.

"I'll be there in a few."

***

"Lady don't scare me like that."

Julius sat at the kitchen table while Savannah fixed him a glass of sweet tea. He'd been really concerned about his sister-in-law and Savannah didn't know it but if she hadn't answered that phone this last time, he had already decided he was going to pop up unannounced just to make sure she was okay.

"You had me thinkin' you done slipped back into some kind of depression."

"I know," Savannah said, sorry that she'd been avoiding him for so long.

She brought the drink over to him and took a seat at the table.

"It's just been crazy, that's all."

Julius took a sip and said, "Well, you know I'm here for you. I know it's tough with Gene bein' in the hospital, but you ain't gotta go through this alone."

Savannah looked at Julius as he genuinely spoke to her. She smiled, slightly. She loved him. She knew he meant what he said, and she knew he wanted the best for her. You would never be able to tell he and Eugene were brothers just by looking at them. Eugene looked more like their mom, and Julius, from his dark skin, to his strong face, and high cheek bones, was a splitting image of their dad. The only thing the two brothers had in common was their height and slim build.

She held up a finger and said, "Excuse me for one minute. I'll be right back."

Savannah got up from the table and went into the den. She had safety left Taylor in her play pin, to play with toys, while she sat with Julius. She picked her up and headed back to the kitchen, with Roxy following close behind.

When she returned, Julius was drinking more of his tea. He stopped for a moment as Savannah sat down with the baby, saying, "That's a pretty baby. Who she belong to? One of yo' friends?"

He didn't wait for an answer as he went on to pat Roxy and say, "Hey Rock," as he called her.

He'd obviously glanced at the baby long enough to see that she was pretty, but Savannah could tell he hadn't really looked at her. If he had, he would have seen Eugene in her. She thought that maybe he was distracted by Roxy. As he took another sip of his tea, Savannah said, "She's Eugene's.

Julius nearly chocked as he quickly sat the glass down. He wiped the tea that had spilled on his dark blue Polo shirt with his hand. Eyes wide, Julius leaned in, as if he hadn't heard Savannah correctly the first time and said, "Say what now?"

Savannah chuckled a little and nodded, saying, "You heard me right. She belongs to your brother."

Julius stared at Savannah in disbelief, longer than he intended to.

"Umm," Julius began, pausing to gather his thoughts, "That's Gene baby," he asked, making sure he'd heard her correctly.

Savannah nodded.

"You mean like, you didn't have nothin' to do with makin' her?"

"Right," Savannah nodded.

"Okay, wait, before I assume anything. I know y'all had been havin' problems with gettin' pregnant so, did y'all decide to do one of those surrogate mother thangs? You know, where you plant the seed in somebody else?"

Savannah chuckled, saying, "Oh, your brother planted a seed alright, but it sure wasn't in my garden."

Julius leaned in closer to get a better look at the baby. Then, he said, "Oh yeah. That's his baby."

Savannah nodded.

Julius, who was still processing the new information, sat back and shook his head.

"Well I'll be."

Savannah watched Julius, quietly, as he stared off into the distance. She could tell he was confused. Still trying to figure out what was what and how was how. She was glad. Glad because she could tell that he knew nothing about Taylor.

"Lord," he said, shaking his head, "That big dummy. I tell you, I wish I could go down there and knock him upside his head and wake his butt up out of that coma."

Savannah chuckled a little.

You and me both, she thought.

Julius suddenly snapped his head up, towards Savannah. He seemed confused.

"Well, Vannah, I have to say, you must of known about this for a while because you seem real calm right now. And the two of y'all," he pointed back and forth between Savannah and Taylor, "Look like y'all the best of friends."

She chuckled again, shaking her head. Then, she went into the whole story about how and when she'd found out and how she got to this point, where she and Taylor had become "the best of friends."

When Julius finally left to return to work, he'd been mad at his brother for making such poor choices, but he was happy to see how well Savannah was handling it. He'd agreed that he would let Savannah tell Eugene about all the darkness that had been exposed. He had asked Savannah how she thought things would be when Eugene returned home, with the baby and her mother living there.

Once again, all Savannah could say was they'd cross
that bridge when they got to it.

Chapter 18

"Man," Tiffany said, a bit frustrated, "This is the third time the manager from the motel has called me."

"What did he say," Savannah said, as she stopped at a red light.

She was minutes away from dropping Tiffany off at the Department of Health Services, because Taylor had a doctor's appointment and she had to pick up some food vouchers for her baby formula.

"He left a message sayin' my stuff would be thrown away if I didn't get it out of the room today. I paid to stay there for a whole month and the month is up today. He said he's gonna give me until 8 pm."

Savannah sighed as she slowly lifted her feet off the brake and eased it onto the gas pedal.

"Do you really need anything that's there?"

"I mean, I would leave it, but I have some important papers like, Taylor's birth certificate and mines and some other stuff."

Savannah wanted to suggest that she just order more of those things, but she didn't want to seem to bossy. Not that that had ever stopped her before. She kept reminding herself that Tiffany was a grown woman and she could do what she liked, but she worried about her running into Jace.

"You wonderin' if Jace will be there, huh?"

Savannah glanced at her and sighed.

She nodded, "Yeah."

"I mean, I doubt he would. I haven't been there in almost three weeks."

"Yeah but, guys like that will take advantage of something until the well runs dry. You don't want to take any chances. I think you should have police escort when you go."

Tiffany frowned a little.

"I don't think it's that serious. I mean…"

"Tiffany," Savannah cut in, "It is that serious. Guys like that are capable of anything. There's no telling what he'll do to you."

Savannah paused, not wanting to overstep her boundaries, again, or get too worked up.

"Well," Savannah said, "Maybe, you could at least let me take you over there to get your things?"

As they pulled up to the front of the office building, Tiffany opened the car door, and as she gathered her things and Taylor, she said, "Okay. I'll call you after I finish and then, we can head over there."

Relieved, Savannah agreed.

"Have a great day," she yelled to her.

"You too," Tiffany yelled back.

Savannah knew that, depending on where she was in the hospital, sometimes reception on her cell phone wasn't that good. Therefore, she wasn't surprised when she'd gotten a voicemail from Tiffany, letting her know that she had tried calling, but it went straight to voice mail. Tiffany also let her know that she had run into an old friend at the office and the friend was going to give her a ride to the motel and bring her home later that evening.

Savannah acknowledged that she had received the voicemail via text and as she sat in her chair, next to her unconscious husband, she said a silent prayer for Tiffany and Taylor, praying that God would protect them both.

***

Tiffany used the key she had to enter the motel room. She slowly turned the knob and peered inside the room, checking to see if there was any other form of human life present. Basically, she was wanting to make sure Jace was not there. She was happy to see that it seemed he hadn't been there, from the way the room looked. The room had been cleaned, as if it were waiting for the next person to occupy it and all of her belongings were in two, big, black, plastic bags, sitting in the corner of the room. She assumed the manager had done that.

She'd left Taylor in the car with her friend because she didn't plan on staying in the room long. Even if her things hadn't been packed, she had only planned on grabbing the things which were most important to her. As she looked through one of the bags, checking to make sure her important papers were in it, she heard the door creak a little. She knew that meant someone was coming in.

She figured it was her friend, so, she yelled over her shoulder to her, saying, "I'm just checking to make sure all my stuff is in here. I'm about to come right out."

"Take your time."

Tiffany froze, and it seemed as if her heart had done the same.

Oh God, she thought.

She slowly turned around. There, standing in the door frame, was Jace. He was holding Taylor, in her car seat, and the baby bag. He sat her on the floor, along with the bag and closed the door. Then, he leaned against it and folded his arms. He didn't say anything. He just stared at Tiffany.

Tiffany's heartbeat quickened as she turned back towards the bags. She nervously gathered the bags and began walking towards the door. She didn't know what his plans were, but she was wishfully hoping that he would just let her walk out of the door. She stopped in front of him.

"Excuse me," she said softly.

He cocked his head to one side and said, "Where you goin'?"

She avoided eye contact with him, saying, "I'm leavin'."

He chuckled, "Clearly. But where you goin'?"

She sighed, "Jace, could you just let me…"

"You goin' to that old lady house," he said, cutting her off. "That rich lady?"

Tiffany didn't say anything. Her eyes had been fixed on Taylor, who sat quietly in her car seat, staring at Tiffany and sometimes, Jace. Tiffany watched how she seemed so attentive. Funny how, until that moment, it had seemed to Tiffany that she had never quite noticed Taylor, the way a mother should. At that moment, Taylor seemed so intuitive. Like, she was following along with the conversation. Like, she could sense that something was wrong.

"Come on, I'll take you over there."

Tiffany had almost been in a trance until Jace made that comment. She looked at him and said, "No, that's okay. I'm gonna have my friend take us."

"Oh, I told her she could leave. I told her I would take you."

Tiffany looked at him and shook her head, "No, it's, it's fine Jace. I'll…"

"What? You don't want me to take you over there? You don't want me to know where you really been? Where you really goin'?"

Tiffany frowned.

"That is where I been," she said. "And you know what, it don't even matter anyway cause I'm leavin'.

Okay? I'm leavin' you and you don't have to deal with me or see me no more."

They stared at each other for a brief moment before Tiffany said, "Now, could you please move so I can go."

"No, I'll take you," he said. "Come on. I got my boys in the car. I know she got some good stuff in that house and a whole bunch of money."

He started to grab the bags from her hands, but she pulled back, saying, "No, Jace."

He pierced his eyes at her.

"You act like you love her or somethin'. She ain't doin' nothin' but makin' you look like a dummy. You over there with this lady and you done had a baby by her husband. What kind of crap is that? She don't care nothin' bout you. She..."

Tiffany was fed up with the way Jace was talking and yelled, "Shut up, Jace! She done more for me than you have ever did. She love us and that's why she took us in. If anything, you the one who makin' me look like a dummy you stupid devil!"

Before she knew it, he yelled, "Shut up," and smacked her hard across the face.

Tiffany fell to her knees. She held her face while Jace yelled at her, calling her anything he could think of.

"You think you better than me now, huh? Cause you been goin' to church? You ain't nothin' but what you been!"

He knelt down in front of her and grabbed her by her hair, forcing her to look at him and said, "And

I'm not asking you no more. You takin' me over her house right now."

He pulled her to her feet by her hair and said, "Get the baby and come on!"

But Tiffany had had enough. She was so tired of him pushing her around. So angry at how she'd let him treat her. So angry at how less of a mother she'd been to Taylor, allowing her to be in the presence of such people.

Savannah had been nothing but kind to her and she refused to let him harm her in anyway. She lunged at Jace, flailing her arms, allowing her fists to land where the fell. The last thing Tiffany vaguely remembered, was hearing the cries of her baby. Jace had punched her with so much force, it caused her to fall backwards, hitting the back of her head on the sharp end of the table.

***

For the remainder of that evening, after Savannah returned home from the hospital, she'd had a continuous, uneasy feeling regarding Tiffany and the baby. She had gotten home after five that evening and she'd waited for three full hours before she tried calling her. After all her calls went unanswered, she regretted not being able to take her to get her things. Yet, she kept telling herself that Tiffany was a grown woman and that everything was alright, trying her best to keep herself from worrying.

But even now, as she lay in bed wide awake, after falling asleep, only to obtain almost three hours of uneasy rest, her troubled spirit had not settled. And at almost 12 in the morning, the unusually loud, unexpected sound of her cell phone ringing, only made her heart skip a beat. Normally, she'd have her cell phone powered off as she slept, but since Eugene had been in the hospital, she kept it on to make sure the hospital could reach her at any time. She sat up quickly, grabbing the phone off the nightstand.

"Hello?"

Savannah answered the phone urgently, unsure of what to expect or who was calling from an unknown number. A deep, but smooth voice filled her eardrum.

"Mrs. Savannah Carmichael?"

"Yes," she answered quickly.

"Hi, Mrs. Carmichael. My name is Detective Miller. I'm with the Atlanta Police Department. In the homicide division."

Homicide, she thought.

"I apologize for calling at this time of night but, I need you to come down to the police station as soon as possible."

There was a brief pause as many questions raced through her mind. Then, Detective Miller stated, "It's about Tiffany Poole."

Although, 90% of Savannah expected the Detective to be calling about something concerning Tiffany, she still didn't know what to expect.

"Tiffany? Is she okay?"

"I'd rather not discuss anything over the phone. It'd be better if you came in."

"Okay," she replied hesitantly.

When she ended the call, she sat on the edge of the bed wondering what could be going on and why did she, of all people, need to come there. She tried her best to read the Detective's tone for any hint of something, but she knew from watching Detective shows that they had a way of saying things while not showing much emotion, even in the worst of situations.

She thought to herself, *Lord, what is it? Maybe Tiffany told them to call me? Did she hurt somebody? Did somebody hurt her?*

Her eyes grew wide as she thought, *What if something happened to baby?*

Fear and anxiety gripped her as she quickly sprang to her feet and put on the first pair of jogging pants and t-shirt she could get her hands on. Then, she hastily pulled on her sneakers, put on a baseball cap and sprinted down the steps, two at a time.

Chapter 19

Detective Miller was a tall, light brown, well-built man, with a smooth, shaven head. He sat on the other side of a black, polished desk, across from Savannah. Just like his voice, the look on his slim, firm face was hard to read. Expressionless.

"Um, Mrs. Carmichael," Detective Miller began.

Savannah grew more concerned as she waited for, what seemed like hours, to hear what he had to say.

"There is never an easy way to say this, but a little after 8 pm, we found Tiffany in a motel room. She's deceased.

"Whaaaat," Savannah said, shocked and deeply concerned.

She shook her head, moaning, "Um, um, um. Lord Jesus."

After taking a moment to process the news, she asked, "What happened?"

He took a deep breath and said, "Well, from the police reports, some of the people staying in the surrounding rooms say they heard a lot of yelling sometime between 5 and 6 pm. Some even said they'd heard a lot of fighting going on from time to time before this incident."

He shrugged his shoulders and said, "For the people who'd been there this last month, they said that the arguing and fighting was not unusual. They claim that after a few minutes, the noise suddenly stopped, but the baby kept crying. Now, normally, a baby crying wouldn't seem strange, but witnesses say the baby continued to cry for almost an hour. Out of concern, one of the people staying there called the manager. When he knocked, no one answered, so he entered the room and spotted the girl lying on the floor. The baby sat next to her, crying. He then called the police."

"Woooow," Savannah said.

She slowly shook her head, feeling sorry for Tiffany. She felt just as equally sorry for Taylor, having to sit there helpless and crying, next to her dead mother.

"Do you know what happened to her," she asked.

"We concluded that she hit her head on the edge of a table because blood was pouring from the back of her head and…"

"Oh, my goodness," Savannah said, placing her hand over her chest.

"And," Detective Miller continued, "There was blood on the sharp end of the table in the room. It doesn't look like this was a slip and fall. Not to mention, the black eye she had looked fresh. It looks more like she was forcefully pushed or hit so hard that she was knocked into it."

Savannah pierced her eyes and whispered, "Jace."

The name left a sour taste in her mouth.

Detective Miller nodded slowly saying, "Yes. Jace. Jace Ramsey. We don't have any solid evidence of anything, but witnesses say they heard him arguing with her at the time all of this was going on so, we can at least place him there at the time of the murder."

"Oh, he did it, alright," she said assuredly.

All she could do was shake her head. Now, she felt even more regretful that she hadn't taken Tiffany to get her things.

With concern in his eyes, Detective Miller said, "Mrs. Carmichael, I know this is hard for you and I hated to have to tell you this, but we always try to reach out to the victim's family first, to let them know what's going on."

Savannah cocked her head. Confused.

"Uh, family," she said, quizzically.

"Yes," Detective Miller nodded. "You are her mother, right?"

Savannah shook her head, a little bewildered, "Her m-m-mother? No, I'm not her mother. Why would you think that?"

Savannah could tell that Detective Miller was so confused and wrapped up in his own thoughts, he hadn't paid any attention to her question. He stared at the floor.

"You know," he said in a whisper, mainly to himself, "I did think it was strange."

He looked at her and said, "Mrs. Carmichael, I've been following your husband's story with this investigation since it happened. Not to mention, we already knew about him from the cases he's handled, and I had never heard of you two having any kids."

He scratched his head.

"I figured I couldn't rule out adoption but..."

He shook his head, in a sort of, snap-out-of-it way, to get back into detective mode and out of confusion mode. Savannah, on the other hand, was still trying to figure out why he would think she was her mother.

"Anyway, I am so sorry to have bothered you with all of this. That's the only reason I was giving you so much information. But you must have some kind of connection to her because..."

The detective was interrupted by a knock at the door. He held up a finger and said, "One moment, please."

Then, he yelled loud enough for the person on the other side of the door to hear him say, "Come in."

Without turning to see who was at the door, Savannah heard a male voice say, "Excuse me,

Detective Miller. Someone from Child Protective Services has just arrived."

"Thanks. Tell them I'll be with them shortly."

After the door closed, Detective Miller said, "Again, Mrs. Carmichael, I sincerely apologize for the misunderstanding and…"

"Wait," Savannah cut him off, "Why is someone from Child Protective Services here? To take the baby?"

"Well," he said, reluctant to further answer any questions about anything involving the case, "Yes, but the child will be alright. It will be placed in foster care until they find a permanent home for it."

Savannah's mind quickly reverted to the horror stories Tiffany had shared with her on some occasions. She thought about the horror that kids who were able to remember things went through. She thought about the kids who were too young to communicate or even comprehend the horror that may be happening to them.

She knew there were good foster and adoptive parents in the world, but for Taylor, the baby that belonged to her husband, how could she let her grow up in the system like her mother did? Especially, now that her mother was forever gone? Especially, when she had the means to care for her?

She would have loved to go home and think long and hard about it. Pray about it, even. Even though, most of the time, the answer is already there. She knew that time was of the essence. Perhaps, that was a good thing.

As Detective Miller got up from his chair, he said, "Well, I'd better go ahead and get with these people, so they can get the baby."

"No," Savannah said, almost under her breath.

He looked at her, unsure of what she'd said, if anything.

"I'm sorry? Did you say something?"

This time, she looked directly at him and said, "No."

Confused, Detective Miller asked, "No?"

"No," Savannah stated again. "She's not going with them. I'm taking her."

Detective Miller had obviously been caught off guard by her statement.

He cleared his throat and said, "Um, Mrs. Carmichael, I understand and honestly, I do appreciate your concern for the child, but I can't just give her to you. I mean, by law there has to, at least be some legal reason for me to give her to you."

"I have a right to have her," Savannah said. Then, quickly added, "Legally."

The Detective shook his head and said, "I'm confused. I thought you said you had no ties to…"

"The baby," Savannah cut in. "I have no ties to Tiffany but th-the baby. Taylor. That's my hus…" She paused. Not by choice, but rather, by force.

Forced, thanks to the hard, imaginary pill that she was now trying to swallow, now that she was speaking the truth out loud.

"That's my husband's baby," she continued.

Ouch. Savannah didn't realize how much those words would sting once they flowed from her mouth.

She quickly added, "The mother is dead and the father, my husband, is in a coma so, that leaves me."

"Legally, I'm her step-mom," she added, softly.

She sat there, in a daze, avoiding eye contact with Detective Miller as the truth continued to deeply sink in.

No doubt, Detective Miller was trying to sort out this puzzle that Savannah had presented to him. He stared at her, quizzically. Slowly, but surely, his face relieved itself of its tension as his mind started putting all the puzzle pieces together. He opened his mouth to speak but nothing came out. He scratched his brow and said, "Wow, um," but no words followed.

"I have all the legal papers you need to see. I have her birth certificate and I have DNA papers proving that Eugene is the Father. I'm his wife so, legally, I can have her. Please, go get her."

Detective Miller bit his bottom lip and nodded his head slowly, agreeably.

"Mrs. Carmichael, this is not to say that I don't believe you, I just have to make sure I stay on top of my job. So, if you can bring the papers proving that she is Eugene Carmichael's, I will gladly release the baby to you."

Immediately, Savannah sifted through her purse and pulled out some papers, handing them to him. She'd had them in her possession from the day she'd gotten them, for no other reason than to torture herself by looking at them every so often. She wanted to see if the results were as she believed she'd seen them. They never changed. Taylor Mignon Carmichael was Eugene Carmichael's baby.

Detective Miller signed heavily after studying the papers. Then, he handed them back to her and as he got up from his chair, he said, "I'll go get it for…"

Savannah snapped, "Her name is Taylor. It's not "it," "the child," or "the baby." Her name is Taylor."

She took a moment to calm herself, giving him an apologetic look.

"Please," she uttered softly, "Call her Taylor."

He nodded, sympathizing with her frustration.

"I'll go get Taylor for you."

As the Detective proceeded to leave, Savannah couldn't shake the question that had been nagging her. Before Detective Miller exited the room, she said, "Detective Miller? I'm still wondering why you thought I was her mom. I mean, why did you call me? Of all people?"

He frowned, pondering on the question. Then, after remembering what triggered his late, night call, he said, "Oh, yeah."

He dug in his pocket and pulled out a business card. He handed it to Savannah, saying, "We found this card in her purse."

Savannah could clearly see that it was one of her business cards that she'd given to Tiffany, but that still didn't reveal why he thought she was her mom. Before the question had a chance to proceed out of her mouth, he flipped the card over and said, "This is what was on the back of it."

Savannah slowly took the card from the clutches of his fingers. She held it before her, staring at the word like it was written in a foreign language. Then, she whispered the word Tiffany had written on the back of the card, as her heart ached sorely for the girl.

"Mama."

***

"I'm so sorry about your mama."

Savannah sniffled, wiping away the tears that kept forming in her eyes. She looked at the precious baby laying on her bed. She'd fed her, bathed her, and now, she lay down sleeping soundly, oblivious to all the things that had transpired. The things that, when she really understood it, would one day rock her world. Savannah could only pray that she would be able to give Taylor the love that she needed to fill any void she may be subject to.

"You know," she said aloud, speaking to God, "It's crazy to think that even with all the bad that's been happening, You knew it would happen like this. I can't help but believe that, as Pastor Larry mentioned before, this crazy situation is somehow working out for my good."

She sighed and shook her head saying, "And not just for my good but Eugene's and Taylor's as well. I mean, we can't have kids and, well, I can't have kids and Taylor doesn't have a mom anymore and..."

She looked at Taylor. She got a little chocked up, trying to hold back her tears.

"Lord, I hate that all of this stuff has happened but thank You. Thank You for Taylor."

Suddenly, her cell phone rang. On an impulse, without looking at the number, she answered the phone, "Hello?"

"Hey, Mrs. Carmichael!"

She knew that accent. It was Tina.

Why is she calling me at this time of morning?

"Hey, Tina. Is everything okay?"

"Yes," she said excitedly. "The other nurses thought it would be too late to call you, but I knew you'd want to hear this."

"Hear what?"

"Your husband! He's awake!"

Chapter 20

It was a little after seven in the morning. Savannah stood stoic in her husband's room, waiting for him to return. She hadn't had a chance to see him yet because the doctors were running tests on him.

She didn't rush to the hospital once she got the call because, firstly, she wanted to freshen up and make herself look presentable. He hadn't seen her in over five months and there was no way she was going to show up looking tired and worn out. Secondly, she had to wait until Tina finished her shift, so that she could watch the baby for her. Although, she thought about telling him about the baby, she didn't want to bombard him with so many things all at once. Especially, after just waking up from being a coma for almost six months.

As she waited, she began to pace back and forth. She decided to sit down because she could tell she was becoming anxious. Only seconds later, she found herself rocking back and forth. She jumped up and went into the bathroom to give herself a once over. She looked in the mirror and finger combed her hair, putting any loose strands in its proper place. She smoothed out her yellow, long-sleeved blouse and removed any lent from her dark, denim pants. Although, she was a heels lady, on this day, she settled for her black, Mary Jane shoes. Cute and comfortable was her aim for today.

As she looked in the mirror, she smiled, just thinking about how excited she was to see him. Then, it suddenly dawned on her that she'd completely forgotten about all the things that had come to past over the last few months. Over the last few hours. She frowned.

"Why am I so excited to see him," she said aloud.

"And why am I trying to spare his feelings when he didn't think about sparing mines while he was out sleeping around and making babies?"

She folded her arms and said, "Oh, I am definitely going to let him know what's going on. I don't care if he did just wake up."

As she began to storm out of the bathroom, she stopped dead in her tracks.

"Where is this coming from, Lord? This-this anger that just swept over me? I mean, I said I forgive him..."

But, she heard, *have you really forgiven him?*

She always found it interesting how the Holy Spirit asked questions that He already knew the answer to. It is such a graceful and humbling way for you to answer the question yourself, so that the truth can set you free. If you're honest.

She couldn't open her mouth to answer audibly. She teared up because she realized she hadn't. She thought she did, but she hadn't. She tried to hold back the tears that were welling up in her eyes, but as she spoke aloud, they pushed their way past her eyelids.

"Father, you have to help me. I want to forgive him. I mean, I don't want to be some bitter person who is trying to act like everything is alright but is really harboring feelings of resentment. I..."

Suddenly, she heard the door to Eugene's room open and a male's voice say, "Mrs. Carmichael?"

She quickly tried to wipe her eyes and face before looking out of the bathroom doorway. It was a doctor she'd seen a few times since Eugene had been there. He was one of the main doctors encouraging her to pull the plug. She wasn't too fond of him. Still, she smiled and said, "Yes?"

"Hi. Eugene is on his way, but I just wanted to give you a heads up. He can't walk too good because his limbs are so weak, therefore, he'll be in a wheelchair. Also, I project that he'll only have to do at least three weeks of physical therapy. You constantly stretching and exercising his body has him in better shape than I've seen in a patient in a long time."

She nodded, smiling weakly, "Thank you, Doctor."

He nodded and said, "You're welcome," before he left.

She knew he could tell that she'd been crying. He just assumed that she was only responding the way any wife or family member would. Happy to see their loved one emerge from a coma.

A few minutes later, after Savannah tried her best to fix herself up, she heard the door to Eugene's room open once again. She heard some chatter, then, she heard an all too familiar voice say, "Where is the love of my life?"

She smiled. Eugene. So cheerful. So loving. So optimistic. Even during the trying or bad times, he always tried to see the bright side of things. Always seeing the glass as half full, even when Savannah saw it as half empty. She began to remember the many things she loved about him. She seemed to have forgotten them over the last few months.

Lord, she thought, *how on earth are we going to get through all this stuff?*

"Vannah," he sang, cheerfully, as he always did on any given day.

She was hurting, but she was still happy, so, she put on a brave face, smiling from ear to ear and stepped out of the bathroom. She was prepared to say something, but she was speechless. Her smile faded as she looked at him, adoringly, as he did her. He placed his hand over his heart and looked her over.

"My, my, my," he said. "You're just as beautiful as I remember."

She giggled a little, remembering how much she loved the way he complimented her. Eugene addressed the two, young, female nurses who Savannah had just realized were in the same room.

"Could you please help me get in bed and give my wife and me some alone time?"

"Yes, sir," they replied.

My wife. Savannah loved to hear him say that. She stood at the foot of his bed, watching as the nurses made him as comfortable as possible. Eugene and Savannah could hardly take their eyes off each other. Neither could they hardly look at each other. They both seemed to be nervous and excited at the same time. Like they were falling in love all over again. Sort of like the shyness one experienced around their crush. It was overwhelming for them both. The nurses excused themselves, giggling as they exited because they could feel the sweet, loving tension in the air.

As Eugene shifted around, making himself more comfortable, he moved over to make room for Savannah. Then, he softly said, "Come lay next to me. Please?"

Savannah strolled around to his bedside. She was nervous. Why? It had been so long since she'd been touched by him. Voluntarily. Since she'd heard his soothing voice. She'd been longing to experience so many of the things they shared together. Eugene may have seemed cool, calm, and collect to her, but on the inside, he was as excited and anxious as a kid on Christmas day.

Savannah climbed into the bed, carefully. They both lay on their sides, facing each other. Neither of them knew what to say. Even Eugene, being as outspoken as he was, didn't know how to break the ice. They only stared at each other, which spoke volumes because both of them could clearly see the love the other held so deep inside.

Finally, Eugene said, "I even missed you while I was sleeping."

That brought bursts of laughter, smiles, tears, hugs, and kisses out of them both.

"Oh, I missed you so much," Savannah said, as they embraced and continuously pecked each other with kisses.

"I know baby," Eugene replied. "I know. I'm so sorry I wasn't here for you. I..."

Savannah cut him off, "No baby, it wasn't your fault. You didn't know this was going to happen."

"I know," he replied, "But I know you had to deal with so much. I mean, you had to handle all the business of the house and I'm not saying you couldn't, but I can only imagine how things have been with this investigation and the media. I know it's been crazy. I'm so sorry."

Tina had already told Savannah that Eugene had been brought up to speed on the murder investigation. His colleagues had come in early that day. Sure, they were concerned about him, but their main concern was finding out where the materials from Susan Galloway had been hidden.

Savannah listened as he earnestly apologized for not being there for her. For her having to deal with so much. Her excitement to see him had made the things that surfaced over the last few months dissipate. But once again, all of the things that she'd forgotten about, the moment she saw him, came flooding back in like a tidal wave.

She stared at him, thinking, *You have no idea what I've had to deal with, Eugene. You're apologizing for all these things, but you have yet to apologize for the thing that's been hurting me the most. Let alone, admit it.*

She had to look away from him because she knew she might lash out. From hurt. From love. From anger.

"Vannah?"

Eugene raised himself up on his forearm.

"Baby, what's wrong?"

Savannah shook her head, not wanting to speak or look at him.

"Vannah," he said, as he placed his hand on her cheek, gently forcing her to look at him. She looked at him through blurred eyes.

Her voice cracked as she whispered, "You just don't know."

"Baby, I know it's been hard…"

"No, Eugene," she cried. "You don't know how hard it's been. You just don't know."

She began to weep, louder than she intended to. Eugene embraced her tightly.

Sure, Eugene knew that he had fathered a child out of wedlock, but right now, at this very moment in time, his act of infidelity and the results of it was far from his mind. Why wouldn't it be easy for him to forget? He had no communication or physical contact with the child. No bond. He'd only seen her once and that was during the DNA testing. He met with the mother once a month to pay her off and he even forgot about that sometimes. That is, until the day of, when the discreet reminder he set on his phone, reminded him of his skeletons.

He never planned on becoming a deadbeat dad. He knew his father and his mother were probably turning over in their grave because of it, but due to the circumstances, he didn't know how to go about handling it. Afraid that his marriage would end, he didn't know how to tell Savannah. There were times when his conscience bothered him immensely and he believed he was ready to let the truth be known, but every time, he reneged.

"I'm so sorry," he whispered.

He repeated it over and over, oblivious to what was really bothering her.

Chapter 21

"Ju!"

Ju. That was the childhood nickname that had been given to Julius by Eugene. Being that Eugene was the younger of the two brothers, he'd always had a hard time saying Julius and "Ju" was the only thing anyone could ever make out. Therefore, it stuck, even in his adulthood.

"Lil' brother, what's up?"

Julius strolled around to the side of Eugene's bed and they gave each other a brotherly hug.

"Nothing much, just happy to be alive, man," Eugene said.

"I know that's right," Julius agreed.

Eugene eyed Julius' attire, admirably.

"What you all dressed up for," he asked.

"Oh," Julius smirked, straightening out his grey tie which lay against his ocean blue collar shirt.

"This," he began, as he removed his grey, pinned striped jacket, "Is something I just picked up yesterday for this court thing I had to go to this morning."

"Court thing?"

Julius hiked up his dress pants that matched his jacket, as he sighed heavily and sat down in the chair next to Eugene's bedside.

"Yeah, man. Remember that lil' short dude I told you I hired almost a year ago?"

Eugene looked off in the distance, thinking, trying to remember who he was referring to.

"You know," Julius added, "The midget?"

"Ooooh, yeah" Eugene said.

"Well, I fired him about three months ago and he sued the company."

"What," Eugene perked up in bed, obviously concerned. "Why? What happened?"

"It's no biggie," Julius said, brushing it off. "He tried to say I was discriminating against him, you know, because he's short. But, I mean, the man was fallin' asleep almost every day, when he was supposed to be workin' and he was takin' forever to get back from his lunch break. He claims it's because of some condition he got but…"

"What condition?"

Julius smacked his teeth and said, "I don't know, some sleeping disorder he said he got. My thing is, you probably don't need to be workin' at a factory where you supposed to be on the line at a certain time."

"Well, what happened," Eugene asked, still concerned.

"Nothin' much. We settled out of court."

"Whaaat. Darn it! I could've beat that."

Julius chuckled at his brother, knowing how competitive he was, especially, when it came to work.

"Anyway," Julius said, changing the subject, "You know when you gone get out of here?"

"Not really," Eugene answered, more relaxed. "The doctor said it could be about two weeks. Depends on how my physical therapy progresses. But they said it could have been longer if it weren't for Savannah massaging and exercising my body."

Julius nodded, admirably.

"Hey, Ju, let me ask you something. How has Savannah been?"

Julius shrugged a little, knowing a good amount of what's been going on, but confused by exactly what Eugene was referring to.

"What do you mean," he asked. "I mean, of course, she been missin' you a lot."

"I know that but," Eugene paused. He bit his bottom lip, deep in thought. Julius could tell something was nagging him.

"I know she's had to deal with a lot with the media and my not being here, awake, but yesterday when she came, she just kind of broke down. It was like she's been having to deal with so much more than I know."

Eugene looked at Julius, searching for some answers.

"Yeah, I know she been missin' you. Think about it," Julius said, "It's been like 6 months since you been in a coma. None of us knew how things would turn out. That'll take a toll on anybody."

"Yeah, you right," Eugene said, although, he didn't sound confident that that's what it really was.

Julius could sense this and no matter how badly he wanted to tell Eugene that Savannah had found out about the baby, he promised her that he'd let her tell him. He was Eugene's brother, but he cherished his brotherly relationship with Savannah as well, so, he held his tongue.

Still, he found it hard to believe that Eugene hadn't thought that maybe, just maybe, the baby is what Savannah could be referring to. He asked, "Is there anything that you can think of that could cause her to be like that?"

Eugene sighed, thinking. Then, he shook his head, saying, "Nope. Nothing I can think of."

Julius knew his brother. He could tell when he wasn't being truthful. And right now, he could tell that thoughts of Taylor and the other woman were far from his mind.

"Um, Gene, you don't have amnesia, do you?"

Although, Julius was being serious, he smirked a little when he said it. He didn't want to seem too serious.

Eugene laughed a little, "Not that I know of. Why you asking…" Eugene paused to yawn in mid-sentence and said, "Woo, excuse me."

"Come in now, I know you not tired," Julius said, changing the subject. "You should feel like a brand-new woman as long as you been sleepin' in that dress you got on."

They both laughed. Eugene knew he was referring to the hospital gown he was wearing.

"Oh, I see you got jokes, huh," Eugene said, laughing.

"Nah, you know I'm playin'. I'm just happy you back, bro."

"I know. Thanks, man," Eugene said.

"But um," Julius began, standing to his feet, "I'm about to go ahead and get out of here. It's been a long day, but I'll be back down here soon, though."

"Alright. Love you, bro."

"Love you too, lil' brother."

Chapter 22

"Savannah, you gotta tell Gene. He come home tomorrow."

It had been ten days since Eugene had come out of his coma and he was due to be released from the hospital in one day. Savannah tapped her fingers on an antique, gold coffee table, which rested next to the sofa. She was exhausted, mentally and emotionally. She'd just come from Tiffany's funeral, where she made sure she kept a low profile, although, it was kind of hard to do.

Even with the black shades and a black hat with a wide brim, that hung over her eyes, there were only seven people in attendance, including her, so, it wasn't like she could blend in with the crowd. There was a black man, a white man, a black woman, and three young girls, one white and two black. Although, she tried, Savannah couldn't accurately guess who the people were. and she could tell they were trying to figure out who she was, as well.

If it hadn't been for Savannah, discreetly arranging Tiffany's funeral, she wondered if she would have even had a funeral or a proper burial. Since Tiffany's death, Savannah had been running around nonstop. She did business with a funeral home located over an hour's drive outside of the city. She bought a plot and a tombstone for her, paying whatever she needed, to make this happen for Tiffany. She did all of this under a fake name, making sure her black shades and wig, which covered part of her face, was always a part of her attire.

After a quick prayer from the pastor in attendance, he asked anyone if they would like to say anything. No one came up. Afterwards, Savannah waited as everyone went to view the body, one by one, to pay their respects. Then, she went up to see Tiffany.

She stared at the young girl, who'd been fixed up beautifully. She lay her hand over her heart as a shot of pain pierced through her own. Then, as tears formed in her eyes, she quickly dashed out of the church doors. Afterwards, Savannah sat idle in her car, waiting for the hearse to load Tiffany up, to transport her to the burial site. Being that she already knew where the gravesite was, she headed over there first. She didn't get out, she simply sat in her car, afar off, watching them as they lowered her into the ground, then, she drove home.

Julius had come over to drop off Eugene's monthly share of the profits from the family business. Julius felt bad for keeping something like this from his brother and there were a few times he almost told him. Not to throw Savannah under the bus but more so, to help her. It seemed like she didn't know how to tell him. Why, he didn't know. It wasn't like she was the one who had cheated.

"I know. I will. I just…"

She breathed deeply. She just…didn't know. She didn't know when she would tell him. She didn't know how to tell him. She didn't even know why she hadn't told him. Before Julius left, she informed him that she would tell Eugene the day he came home. Julius let her know that he'd bring him home. She was so thankful for that.

After Julius left, Savannah continued busying herself around the house. She'd put Taylor down for a nap an hour ago and she planned to wake her up in a little while so that they could go grocery shopping for some of Eugene's favorite foods. As she hung up some clothes that had been resting on the baby blue chaise in her room, it frustrated her that she found it so hard to tell him about something that was his own doing. She began to feel like it was her secret. Like, she was the one hiding something. She knew she had to tell him. But how?

Maybe, I could pick a fight with him. Not a big one, just something that would give me a reason to lash out at him and tell him about Taylor?

She thought for a moment. Then, she quickly shook her head and chuckled to herself.

"How immature is that, Savannah," she said aloud.

She knew that if he'd been conscious when this first came to light, she would have confronted him then and there, no questions asked, but it didn't work out like that. Perhaps, this situation needed to be handled gracefully, after the anger and the hurt and all the emotions that came with it had subsided. At least, as much as she believed they did. She sighed heavily.

"Lord, just help me say it. Give me the grace and the right words to say."

***

Eugene inhaled deeply as he stood in the doorway of his home.

"Umm. It smells good in here."

He was referring to the smell of sweet potatoes, rosemary, garlic, and many other seasonings and aromas.

"It does smell delicious in here," Julius agreed, who'd just come in behind him, carrying an overnight bag.

Sounds of Vivaldi filled the air as Eugene hobbled towards the kitchen. He called out, "Vaaannaaah?"

Even though, the doctors, as well as, Savannah, insisted Eugene continue to use a wheelchair, just until he was able to stand firmly on his own, he was persistent. Determined. He was not going to sit in a wheelchair and be pushed around or waited upon by anyone. Everyone figured out that they wouldn't win that battle so, they let it be.

As Eugene entered the kitchen, with Julius trailing behind, making sure his brother was stable, he said, "There she is."

Savannah looked up, smiling. She carefully sat a casserole dish, filled with baked chicken, on the marble countertop, then, she walked towards him.

Her stylish, gray, oversized, silk dress swayed with every movement. She'd started to put on some kind of stylish shoes to go with it but decided against it. She went for comfort instead, wearing a pair of black sandals which showed off her freshly, painted toes.

She cupped his face in her hands and planted a kiss on his lips. Then, he gave her a one-armed hug as she hugged him, careful not to cause him to lose his balance.

Savannah thanked God for Tina. She'd agreed to keep Taylor overnight so that Savannah and Eugene could have a talk. A talk that Savannah was dreading, for many reasons but one that desperately needed to happen.

Savannah broke their embrace and headed back over to the casserole dish. As she took it to the dining table, Julius said, "Well, "I'm going to get out of here and leave you two love birds alone."

"You sure you don't wanna eat with us, bro," Eugene asked. "It's gonna to be good."

"Oh, I know," Julius replied. "But I'm gonna leave you two alone. I'm sure you both have some catchin' up to do."

Being that Eugene was getting himself situated at the dinner table, he didn't see the exchange of looks Savannah and Julius had given each other.

***

"I'm so happy."

Savannah looked up from the salad that she'd picked around. Her eyes met his. She smiled, softly.

"I know."

She was happy too. Which is why she dreaded having this discussion. Call her selfish, but the main reason she prolonged having the talk was because she didn't want to dampen the mood. Yet, she knew she had to do it. What bothered her most, was how this "truth" would play out afterwards.

Lord, help me, she thought.

Eugene perked up and said, "We should take a trip somewhere. Somewhere far and for a good length of..."

Savannah cut him off, "Eugene?"

He looked at her. He removed his knife and fork from his chicken, letting them rest on his plate. He sensed the seriousness in her tone, with a hint of worry on her countenance. After wiping his mouth with his beige, cloth napkin, he lay it beside his plate, giving her his full attention.

"What is it," he asked, unsure of what to expect.

She looked away from him. She exhaled heavily, trying to think of where to start and how to bring it forth. She couldn't come up with any way which seemed good enough.

Just say it, she thought.

She picked up a small, black remote, used to control the stereo and stopped the music from playing. She turned to him and said, "Eugene, I, I know about the baby. I know about Taylor."

Chapter 23

Eugene sat back in his chair. He folded his hands behind his head, looking towards the ceiling. Savannah had hit him hard with something that he'd completely forgotten about.

How could I have forgotten about that, he thought. *Perhaps, I didn't want to remember.*

He slowly let his elbows fall to the table. Then, he interlocked his fingers, resting his chin on them. He glanced at Savannah, who'd gone back to picking over her salad. He was trying to read her mood. He didn't know how she'd found out or when she'd found out. He wondered about that because she seemed way too calm about it all. Like she'd already had time to deal with the surprise of it all.

He cleared his throat and said, "How- how long have you known?"

"Almost three months," she replied dryly.

He nodded slowly.

"How?"

She looked at him, "She came to the hospital demanding the money that you'd been paying her to keep quiet."

This time, her response held more hurt. More accusation. He looked around, fidgety. He wasn't sure what to say or what she wanted him to say. He didn't want to say anything to trigger any angry emotions. He was somewhat, afraid. Nervous, even. Nervous and afraid because she was so calm. Perhaps, that was a good thing.

He cleared his throat, "Savannah, I- I'm sorry. It-it didn't mean anything. It just, sort of, happened."

She looked at him. He wanted to kick himself as soon as those last words left his mouth. He was one of the main people who always mocked others when they made comments like that. Savannah rolled her eyes. She folded her arms across her chest and stared at the wall in front of her. It was obvious he didn't know what to say, so, she decided to let him in on just how much she was really involved in Taylor's life.

She spoke stoically, saying, "Tiffany and Taylor have been leaving here for almost a month now."

Eugene's head snapped towards Savannah. He looked at her, bewildered.

"And Tiffany," she continued, allowing the words to fall from her mouth without hesitation, "Eleven days ago she was..." her voice trailed off.

She hated having to bring up the tragedy. She cleared her throat and continued, "Eleven days ago she was killed by her boyfriend."

Eugene gasped, in shock.

"Therefore," Savannah continued, "I've had Taylor full time since then. They were staying in the room downstairs, but since Tiffany...I moved Taylor's room upstairs."

Wow, Eugene thought.

He was at a loss for words. He buried his head in his hands. Suddenly, he looked up at Savannah.

"Is that what you meant at the hospital? I didn't understand why you were so upset but that's what it was, wasn't it? That's what you meant by me not knowing about all that you've had to deal with? Isn't it?"

The emotionless, sideways look Savannah gave him let him know he was right.

"Wow. Vannah. I'm so, so sorry, baby. I…"

"You already said you were sorry, Eugene."

She snapped at him, although, she hadn't meant to. She started to apologize but decided against it.

I'm not the one who should be apologizing, she thought.

Eugene swallowed hard, asking, "Is she here? The baby?"

"No. The nurse, Tina, is keeping her overnight."

He nodded.

"Is there anything you want to ask me?"

Even though, he didn't want to and hadn't planned on spending his first day back home talking about his infidelity, he thought that would be the best thing to say since it seemed like she had more information than he did. He loved his wife and he didn't plan on losing her. Not now. Not ever. He was willing to answer any questions she had for him.

Savannah glanced over to him. Although, she had questions, she was drained. She didn't want to talk about nor hear any of the details about his little fling with another woman. And now, as she predicted, the mood had been dampened. For her, anyway. She sighed exhaustively as she arose from her chair.

"It's alright," she said, looking away from him. "I honestly didn't want to bring it up but," she looked at him, "I had to. It was draining me."

He nodded, understanding what she meant.

"I'm really tired, though," she said. "I'm going to take a bath and lie down."

As she started to leave, she turned back to him and asked, "Will you be alright, or do you need my help with anything."

He shook his head, "No. I'll be alright. Thank you."

She nodded and turned to leave.

He called to her, "Savannah."

She slightly turned towards him.

"I love you."

She hesitated. He couldn't see the water well up in her eyes, due to the dim lighting, but he did hear a slight crack in her voice as she replied, "I love you too."

Then, she walked away. He wanted to run after her. He wanted to catch up with her and pull her into his arms and love on her. He cursed himself. He hated that he had to depend on crutches. He hated that he couldn't go to her as quickly as he wanted to. He hated that he couldn't go back in time. He hated that she had to deal with so much by herself and most of all, he hated that he'd been the cause of her pain.

He watched her walk away and disappear around the corner. Out of his life. It seemed.

Chapter 24

The day Tina brought Taylor home, Eugene found himself at his most uncomfortable state ever. He couldn't bring himself to reach out to her. To hold her. To touch her. He couldn't even bring himself to say so much as, "Hi."

Ove the next few weeks, there hadn't been much interaction between anyone, except, Savannah and Taylor. Eugene had been studying how Savannah interacted with her. How well she treated her. She treated her with such genuine love and so much patience. She took up so much time with her. She treated Taylor like she was her own child. Not as a woman who resented the child and ignored them because of their own bitterness.

No. She didn't treat Taylor that way. But, to Eugene, that's how she was treating him. Ever since Taylor had returned home, Savannah seemed more distant. It confused him. She'd been so happy at the hospital, as well as, the day he came home. Now, she hardly held a conversation with him unless she had to and even then, her answers were very short. Even her body language was different. They had slept in the same bed every night and every night, Savannah found some excuse as to why she wouldn't let Eugene love on her.

He was ashamed to admit it, but he was the one who resented the child. He resented her because of the attention she was receiving from his wife. He resented the obvious bond they shared with each other. The bond they obviously formed while he was away, sleeping. But why? Why was he feeling like that about a child? About his own child?

He should have been happy. Ecstatic, even. To know that his wife had accepted the child that he'd fathered with another woman. Yet, he wasn't, and he didn't know why, but he knew it was a problem.

***

The sun had just begun to set on a cool, Friday evening, when Eugene asked Savannah, "Are we going to church Sunday?"

He'd been trying his best to make small talk as they all sat around in the sunroom, enjoying the nice Spring weather in early May. Eugene sat on a lounge chair, reading his newspaper, or at least, acting like it as he watched Taylor and Savannah.

Taylor sat in her play pin, surrounded by the toys and stuffed animals she was playing with while Savannah, changed out flowers from the many flower pots she had sitting and hanging around.

Savannah didn't look up from the flowers she was arranging in a small, ceramic, flower pot as she casually said, "You haven't said one word to her. You haven't even touched her."

She finally looked at him and said, "Why?"

He looked up from the newspaper he wasn't really reading and shook his head, acting confused as if he didn't know what she was talking about. He stammered over his words.

"I don't...what are you..."

"Oh, come on, Eugene," she cut him off.

"You haven't said one word to your own child. I mean, I'm the one who should be as resentful and withdrawn as you are."

She stood with one hand on her hip. He knew this was a serious moment, but he could hardly keep his focus as his eyes drifted over the curves of her body. The floral, button up dress she had on accentuated them and it was just short enough to reveal those long legs he loved so much.

"Eugene!"

He snapped out of the trance he hadn't realized he was in. He signed heavily, more from frustration.

"Savannah, I..."

He shook his head, confused.

"I can't explain it," he continued. "I don't know why I don't feel something for the child."

He threw up his hands, shrugging.

"I just don't know," he said.

He let his hands fall back by his sides, feeling ashamed by even admitting that.

"Maybe if you'd stop ignoring me and treat me like I'm your husband, the atmosphere would change around here."

"Don't you dare make this about you and don't you dare try to act like you're the victim. If anything, *we*," she pointed to Taylor, then, herself, "Are the victims."

"Baby, I know," he calmly said as he got up and walked over to her.

Although, there was still a slight limp present, he was so happy that his persistence and determination of ridding himself of crutches had paid off in only a few weeks.

He gently placed his hands on her shoulders and said, "Vannah, I'm not trying to play the victim, but we've been here for over a month together and you still haven't allowed me to know you as my wife again. I mean, come on, baby, why are you doing me like this?"

She slightly rolled her eyes at him and smacked her teeth. Once again, he had a hard time staying focused on the situation at hand. He loved when she had a little attitude with him. He'd playfully joke with her to get her laughing and then, she'd be over it. Of course, the attitudes she had never came from something of this nature, but he figured, why not give it a try.

"Come on, boo," he said in a playful way. "You know I loooove you."

He smiled, but she didn't. Still, he leaned in to try to kiss her and she turned away from him.

"Savannah," he whined, as he let his hands fall by his side.

"You know why I don't want you to touch me," she asked, seriously.

Before he could answer, she looked at him and said, "Because every time I think about letting you touch me, all I see is the two of you together."

He hated the hurt he saw in her eyes, but it was there.

"Savannah, baby, I..."

She cut him off, "I bet if Taylor hadn't emerged from all of this, I wouldn't have found out about your little fling, would I?"

She stared at him, with daring eyes.

"Would I have found out, Eugene?"

He tried to speak calmly, saying, "Savannah, it wasn't a fling, I just..."

"Would I have found out," she repeated, cutting him off.

He tried to speak, but she cut him off again, more demanding.

"Would I have found out or not!?"

"I don't know," he yelled.

They stared at each other, both hurt by their own hurts.

"I don't know, Savannah," he calmly said.

He reached for her hand.

"Baby. I'm so sorr..."

She took a quick step back so that he couldn't touch her.

"How many other women have you cheated on me with?"

Pleadingly, he said, "Vannah, please don't do that. You know I haven't been with anyone else?"

She looked at him with disgust and scoffed.

"Excuse me? Please don't tell me what I know. I don't know who you've been with, Eugene. I didn't even know that you would do something like this. Or even, think about being with another woman. Don't you dare tell me what I know because I obviously don't know as much as I thought I did."

Frustrations were running high as he said, "Okay, Savannah, I'm sorry. I made a mistake. What do you want me to do?"

"Oh no, boo," Savannah said with attitude as she rolled her neck and wagged her finger in his face.

"That was not a mistake. A mistake would be you going to the store to buy cottage cheese, when I told you to buy sour cream. That's a mistake. You don't just make a mistake and sleep with someone other than your wife. What you decided to do, took time to process in your mind and in your heart. What you decided to do, determines our future together. *That* is so much more than a mistake."

He was taken aback.

"Determines our future together? Wh-what do you mean? What are saying?"

She looked away from him and took a few more steps back.

"I just," she sighed. "I think I need some time away from you."

She looked at Eugene, who was baffled. He couldn't find the words to say and neither did Savannah wait for him to gather his thoughts. She quickly headed into the house, stopping for a split second when she saw Taylor looking up at them. She'd forgotten she was even in the room. She'd been so quiet and surprisingly unaffected by it all.

Savannah speedily walked to their room. Eugene followed as closely as he could, trying his best to get her attention. She moved around the room, gathering clothes from the drawers and some of her other essentials, stuffing them in her small suitcase. Eugene slowly sat down on the bed, watching her in disbelief. As she finished her packing and started for the door, he stood up, blocking her way.

"Savannah, baby, we can work this out."

She didn't respond, at least, not to his pleading.

"There is plenty of formula in the pantry and the diapers are in the closet, in her room," she said. "If you run out of those things, I suggest you go buy more."

She didn't wait for him to move out of her way. She pushed past him and made her way down the steps. Eugene followed closely behind her.

"Can you at least tell me where you're going?"

She didn't respond. As she inched towards the door, he said, "Savannah, please don't go."

She opened the door to leave, but he gently grabbed her arm and stopped her. He placed his hands on her cheeks, so he could look at her and she'd be forced to look at him.

"Vannah, please. Stay. Please."

As she stared at him, she could clearly see the hurt in his eyes. The love.

God, I love this man, she thought.

She quickly looked away.

"I pray," she began, trying to gather her thoughts and keep herself from crying, "I pray that the Lord softens your heart towards your daughter. But I, I just," she shook her head and threw up her hand. "I can't do this."

She quickly pulled away from him, making her escape to her car. She tossed her things in and climbed into the driver's seat. As she started the car, she was thankful for her tinted windows and the night sky, which kept the tears that were now streaming down her face, a secret.

As she backed down the driveway, she couldn't help but glance at him, standing on the doorstep. He looked so helpless. Powerless. He knew there was nothing he could do and obviously, nothing he could say to make her stay. He watched her drive away, as his own tears began to give way.

Chapter 25

It was a little after 10 pm as Savannah hit the ignore button on her cell phone, once again, for the 9th time. She knew who it was, and she was not going to answer it or respond to his messages. She also deleted the text messages upon arrival because she knew that if she read them, she'd be tempted to respond.

"I bet he's going out of his mind over there," Tina said, as she poured both, Savannah and herself, another cup of tea.

"Not knowing where you are must be killing him," she added.

Tina handed Savannah a green, ceramic tea cup and joined her on the rose, colored sofa.

"Thank you."

She took a sip of the cup's hot contents and said, "I hated to leave her there. Him too," she admitted.

"Well, why did you leave her?"

Savannah rubbed her head.

"There are just so many reasons, Tina. I don't know, I just, I can't be around him right now. He hasn't even touched the child or said one word to her.

Since *you* brought her home that day. I don't know what's wrong with him. I guess I'm hoping that leaving her with him will somehow force him to deal with her and the rest of his demons."

Tina nodded, understandingly.

"Are you going back to him," Tina asked.

Savannah knew that she loved her husband, but that was a question she had asked herself over and over, since she'd left. The truth was..., "I don't know," she said.

She groaned, saying, "I love him. So much. I think that's why I'm having such a hard time dealing with it."

She shook her head and said, "I just can't be there right now."

"Well," Tina began, as she patted Savannah on the leg, assuredly, "You know you're welcomed to stay here as long as you like."

With a slight smile, Savannah nodded.

Tina giggled saying, "He's probably going crazy over there. What's he gonna do all by himself with that baby?"

"I don't know, and I really don't care. He better figure it out. If he got any sense, he better call on the Lord for some help."

They both laughed as Tina said, "You right about that."

***

Eugene scratched his head as he stood over the play pin, staring down at Taylor. She'd been pretty patient, but he could tell her patience was wearing thin. He knew exactly why. The smell that was coming from her had hit him in the nose like a ton of bricks. He knew she needed to be changed.

He sighed heavily and shook his head saying, "Lord, please, help me."

As a sudden thought came to him, he quickly reached in his pocket to retrieve his cell phone. He called someone whom he knew had more experience than he did when came to dealing with kids.

"Hey," he said, mildly panicked. "I need you to come over, asap. Please."

He ended the call and for the next ten minutes or so, he paced back and forth. He paced back and forth from the sunroom, where Taylor was, to the living room, where he looked out of the window every so often.

Taylor had just begun to whimper a little, therefore, he was relieved when he saw headlights flash in front of the window. He snatched open the door and yelled, "Hurry up, bro!"

"What's goin' on," Julius asked, once he'd hurried over to him, concerned.

"Come on."

Eugene closed the front door and led him to the sunroom. He gestured towards Taylor and said, "You have to help me with this."

Julius, confused, looked at Taylor, then, back to Eugene and asked, "Help you with what?"

Eugene looked at Julius as if he'd lost his mind, saying, "You don't smell that?"

Julius smacked his teeth and said, "Maaaan, I know you didn't get me out of bed for this. I thought somethin' bad had happened."

"I just figured you would know what to do. I mean, you do have like 20 kids," Eugene said, with a slight smile.

Julius, who didn't think it was funny at all, rhetorically asked, "I been up since 4 this mornin', tendin' to the family business, and you rush me over here to change a diaper?"

Eugene sighed, "It's not like that Ju. I just..."

Eugene rubbed his temples.

"I need help."

He threw his hands up saying, "I don't know what I'm doing."

Still not satisfied with the answers he was receiving, Julius frowned, asking, "Well, where's Savannah? Why can't she do it?"

Eugene looked away from Julius, toward the ground. He grabbed onto the rim of the play pin. He gripped it hard as if he needed it to hold himself up.

He looked at Taylor as he said, "She," he cleared his throat, "She left."

He then, looked at Julius and said, "Savannah left me."

Julius' face softened. Then, he said, "Show me where her stuff is."

"So," Julius began, as he sat in the rocking chair, holding Taylor, "Are you gone try to get your wife back or you just gone let her leave like that?"

Eugene, who sat on the floor with his back against the wall, tightened his jaw as he shook his head saying, "I don't know."

"You don't know," Julius repeated.

"I mean, of course, I won't her back. I want her here, right now but..."

Julius cut him off saying, "Do you think she wants to come back?"

That was what scared Eugene the most. It was also something he didn't know the answer to.

He cleared his throat and said, "I can't say. I'm hoping she just needs some time alone, you know?

Some time to process everything. There's obviously been a lot going on and I know she's been dealing with a lot..."

His voice trailed off as he quickly shook his head, not wanting to think about Savannah not coming back.

"I know she loves me," he added.

"Yes," Julius nodded in agreement, "I can clearly see that. But," he looked down at the baby and said, "A baby. A situation like this. That'll rock any woman to the core."

He then, looked up at Eugene, through sincere eyes and said, "I've had some good women in my life, bro. Some real good women."

He shook his head and looked back down towards the baby. He gave her something to drink from her sippy cup.

Eugene knew that Julius was speaking about the things that he'd dealt with. On two occasions, he'd had another baby with someone else, while he was in a relationship. At first, Eugene started to discount what he was saying. He loved his brother dearly, but he knew how he was. He knew that he was the "playa" type. Never the one to get serious enough with a woman to want to be faithful to her, let alone, make her a wife.

Eugene believed that his situation was different than his brother's. He and Savannah had been together for a long time. Married. Eugene had never cheated on Savannah before and, as far as he believed, neither had she. But, there was something about the way Julius looked. Something about the way he had made those statements let Eugene know that he understood. He could relate and even though, he wasn't married to any of these women, there must have been some kind of love there. Even, if it wasn't the kind that a husband and wife shared.

Whether Eugene messed up one time, or five times, it didn't make him any better than Julius. He messed up and he had to accept that. Yet and still, the last thing Eugene was going to do was entertain the thought that Savannah may not come back. He'd give her some time.

"She beautiful bro," Julius said, bringing Eugene back to reality.

"You knew about her, huh?"

Julius locked eyes with Eugene.

"When I was at the hospital," he continued, "And I made that comment about Savannah and how it seemed like something more was bothering her. You already knew about the baby?"

Julius sighed, "I had promised Savannah I would let her tell you."

"It's cool, man," Eugene said. "I understand."

He chuckled saying, "I knew you had to know something by how calm you were when you saw her, but it shouldn't have had to be your burden anyway. It shouldn't have had to be Savannah's either."

Eugene watched how Julius stared at Taylor, with such admiration. How he handled her as he lay her upon his shoulder to burp her. He watched how it seemed like it came so natural to him. He wondered why it seemed like everyone could do that, but him.

"You know," Eugene began, "I haven't been able to touch her or even talk to her since she's been here. I've hardly looked at her."

"Why you think that is?"

Eugene was almost at a loss for words as he said, "I really don't know. It seems like it comes so natural to everyone. I don't know if it's because I know that I am to blame for everything and maybe I just can't accept the truth. I don't know."

"You know," Julius began, "I remember when you two were dealing with the miscarriages and Savannah's depression. It seemed like goin' to church and talkin' with your Pastor helped a lot. Have you thought about goin' to God about it?"

Eugene frowned a little and looked at Julius sideways. Julius knew why. He hadn't gone to church since they had to bury their parents, almost ten years ago, and before that, since he was a teenager. And that was only because their parents made them go. Anytime Eugene and Savannah invited him to church, he always made up some excuse as to why he didn't want to go. Now, to hear him talk in such a way, caught Eugene off guard.

Julius chuckled saying, "I know, I know, God was not in my vocabulary, but," Julius paused for a brief moment and then, looked at Eugene and said, "While you were in a coma, I had a little scare and..."

"A scare," Eugene cut in.

Julius modestly said, "I had a mild heart attack but..."

"A heart attack," Eugene cut in again, obviously surprised by his admission. "Why didn't you tell me? Did Savannah know? I mean, when, why, why didn't you tell me?"

"Gene, calm down. I'm fine. Besides, I thought it was best not to tell you just yet. I mean, you had just come out of a long coma and you were goin' through your physical therapy and with everything else goin' on with the baby it was, it was just best not to tell."

Eugene looked down, sorrowfully. He shook his head. So much had gone on while he was sleeping. So many people were hurting. Some by his own faults and others, not. And now, there was a baby involved. His baby. And he couldn't even touch her. He felt so hopeless.

"Listen," Julius said, "I'll stay the night and I'll take off tomorrow to watch her for you, but you have to go talk to your Pastor tomorrow. I don't know how to help you with what you dealin' with on the inside, but one thing I do know is that this baby need you."

Eugene nodded slowly, appreciating his brother. Carefully, Julius got up from the rocking chair and sat Taylor in her crib. Then, he walked over to Eugene, held out his hand, and said, "Come on, little brother. Let's pray."

Chapter 26

Bright and early, Monday morning, with a sense of urgency, Eugene hustled through the glass, double doors of Yeshua House Church. He didn't know if he had to make an appointment or not to talk to Pastor Larry, and he didn't care. He had to talk to him.

"Pastor Larry is in a meeting with someone right now and," the petite lady who sat behind the computer screen paused, as she looked down at her computer, then, back to Eugene and said, "And it looks like he's booked for the rest of the day. You'll have to make an appointment."

Eugene groaned in frustration.

"Well, could you at least call him and tell him that Eugene Carmichael really needs to see him, please? It's really important."

"I'm sorry, sir but I'm not entitled to change his schedule and as I said before, he's booked for the day. You'll have to make an appointment."

Eugene sighed. He didn't want to make an appointment. He needed to talk to him. To someone who could give him some answers. To someone who was closer to God than he was.

He looked at the brown-skinned lady, who stared at him, over the rim of her glasses, waiting for an answer. Then, he stormed off towards the closed door, leading to the office of Pastor Larry.

"Sir, you can't go in there" the lady yelled after him.

Eugene, who proceeded as if he didn't hear the lady, barged into his office, saying, "Pastor Larry, I'm sorry but..." his voice trailed off as he spotted Savannah, sitting in one of the two accent chairs. She looked his way and quickly, turned her face away from him. He could tell, without a doubt, she'd been crying.

The secretary appeared at the door protesting urgently, "Pastor Larry, I'm sorry, I told him that he could not come in here and he just barged his way in anyway."

Pastor Larry help up his hand and calmly said, "It's alright, it's alright, Mrs. Fidel. I know you were doing your job. Thank you. I'll handle it."

Eugene, with his eyes still fixed on Savannah, didn't see the lady roll her eyes at him as she left.

"Savannah, why...," Eugene began.

"Eugene," Pastor Larry stopped him. "You can't just barge your way into my office anytime you feel like it."

Embarrassed, Eugene replied, "I know Pastor. I, I apologize but I really need to talk to you. It couldn't wait and," he looked at Savannah, "It must be meant for me to be here because my wife is..."

"You know what, Pastor," Savannah said, as she quickly hopped up from the chair, "I think it's time for me to go."

"Savannah, why haven't you been answering any of my calls or texts," Eugene asked.

She ignored him as she straightened out her long, black, floral print dress. She gathered her purse and Pastor Larry stood up saying, "Savannah, you don't have to go. This is *your* appointed time," he eyed Eugene.

"No," she insisted, "I'll go."

"Well, why can't we talk to him together," Eugene asked her.

She continued to ignore him as she put on her sunglasses.

"Savannah," he persisted, "Let's talk to him together."

Savannah snapped at him, "This is not a couple's session, Eugene."

She sighed, trying to calm down as she turned toward the pastor, saying, "Pastor Larry, thank you, but I have some things to do anyway. I'll be in touch."

"Are you sure, Savannah," Pastor Larry asked.

"Yes, sir, I'm sure. Thank you."

She hurried out of the door, catching a glimpse of Mrs. Fidel's stare. She knew she'd heard what was going on. Maybe she didn't know *exactly* what was going on, but she speculated that they were on bad terms and that they must not be around each other at the moment. That made Savannah even more mad at Eugene for barging in like that. Eugene started after her.

"Eugene," Pastor Larry called out to him, stopping him in his tracks.

Eugene turned towards him.

"Please, have a seat."

"But, Savannah's here. I can go talk to her and…"

"I think it would be best if you left her alone."

Eugene looked towards the door, pondering on whether he should chase after Savannah or not.

"Please, close the door," Pastor Larry said.

Hesitantly, Eugene shut the door and sat down. Pastor Larry loosened the beige tie around his cream colored, collar shirt and hiked up the inseams of his brown, khaki pants as he sat down. He then sat back in his chair and folded his arms across his chest. Then, he looked at Eugene, waiting.

"What," Eugene asked.

Pastor Larry through up his hands saying, "You tell me. Obviously, something couldn't wait."

Eugene interlocked his hands and fiddled around with his thumbs. He looked up to speak and then, he looked towards the ground. He really didn't know what to say. He was hoping Pastor Larry would start the conversation.

Finally, Eugene spoke, saying, "Did, did she say anything about me? You know, like, if she was going to come back or not or…anything?"

Pastor Larry looked at him as a father would do a child and said, "Eugene, you know I can't discuss that with you."

"I know, I just," he inhaled and exhaled loudly, "I just need some help."

He spoke urgently, gesturing with his hands, saying, "I need some answers. I don't know what to do and then, this baby and, uugh! You have to help me. I can't lose my wife. I mean, could you just talk to her. I know she'll listen to you, I just..."

"Eugene," Pastor Larry sternly interrupted him, "Listen to me. I am only a vessel that God is using to reach and teach the people that He loves, and I am grateful for that position. I am also grateful that you and this congregation trust me enough, to come to me, with all your problems. But I say this as humbly as possible. *I* am not the answer. Jesus is the answer."

Eugene signed from frustration and got up. He began to pace back and forth.

Pastor Larry, seeing his frustration, said, "Now listen, Eugene. I know you probably don't want to hear that, but I'm going to keep it as real as I possibly can. What you are seeking is some *right now* answers. Some *right now* solutions. Almost like a quick fix and, although, we serve a present, *right now God*, there are times when we have to endure. There are times when we have to go through the situation that has been presented to us. Sometimes, these situations are presented to us forcibly and sometimes, they are brought on by our very own choices. Now, I can't give you a quick fix for something like this, but if I could, what would you have learned from it? Nothing."

Eugene stood still with his eyes fixed on the many pictures on the wall. Even though, he wasn't looking at Pastor Larry, he was listening.

"Now," he began, with more compassion in his tone, "I do believe, in my heart, that you love your wife and that this is something you wish, with everything in you, that you could take back, but," Pastor Larry leaned forward and asked, "Eugene, could this be a way for you to get closer to God? To know more of Him? To know more of Jesus? To know more of the Holy Spirit? Could the God, who loves you so much, regardless of what you did, be waiting for you to seek Him and cry out to Him? How will we ever grow if we never go through things? Even the things which are a result of our own choices?"

Eugene finally looked towards Pastor Larry.

Coyly, Eugene asked, "What should I say to Him?"

Pastor Larry causally shrugged as he sat back in his chair, "Whatever you want. He's your best friend. He can decipher and understand you better than you can understand yourself. Just start talking. Talk about whatever it is that's on your mind. He already knows what you're thinking before you say it anyway, so you might as well be honest with Him. When you can be honest with God, you will be set free from so many things. Just ask Him to help you. Trust me, brother, he can't wait to help you."

Eugene put his hands in his pocket and looked toward the ground. He then, spoke as if he were ashamed, "The-the baby," he slowly shook his head.

"I can't even bring myself to..."

"Eugene," Pastor Larry cut in, "Talk to the Lord about it. I can't promise anything about any human being, including myself, but I can promise that the Lord will give you all that you need."

Eugene nodded in understanding.

"Now," Pastor Larry said as he got up from his seat and walked towards Eugene, "Before you go, I have to say this because the Holy Spirit is really urging me to say this to you. Ask God to help you to not fall into temptation. Demons are always working against us, but when they know there's trouble, in any situation, they work overtime. Speak only life, not death, over this situation."

Pastor Larry smiled and said, "Let us pray."

The prayer helped Eugene feel a little more at ease about everything going on. No doubt, he still desperately wanted his wife back and his household fixed, but he decided that he ought to give God a try. Especially, seeing that Savannah didn't even want to see him, let alone, speak to him. He felt that he was all out of options.

Chapter 27

"Uugh!"

Savannah got in her car and slammed the door shut. She'd been livid with Eugene for showing up at the church like he did. She started her car and drove off, out of the church parking lot, faster than she intended to.

"I can't believe him," she said aloud to herself.

"The nerve of him bursting in Pastor Larry's office like that. He should really be ashamed of himself. And then, I wasn't even finished talking. Ugh!"

She hated how Eugene could get under her skin like that.

"What am I even talking about our problems...my problems, to Pastor Larry for? I don't even think I want to go back home. I couldn't stand seeing him just then and you know what, I don't think I want to see him ever again. So there!"

She drove down the highway, driving faster than she realized, switching from lane to lane. She thought about how another driver may think she was crazy, arguing with herself. Then again, she thought they'd probably assume she was fussing at someone on a hands-free phone.

She got off the highway, heading towards the Crowne Plaza hotel she'd just checked into that morning. She adored Tina and she knew she could stay at her place as long as she needed to, but Tina had a house full living with her. Although, Tina worked long hours at the hospital, between her two daughters and their eight kids, Savannah knew she'd never have as much peace as she wanted being there.

She turned off the ignition and sat in the car. She burst into to tears.

"I'm so tired of crying," she yelled.

She looked up and said, "I'm tired of my emotions getting the best of me. I'm tired of not knowing how I'm going to feel the next day. I'm just tired. I'm tired of everything."

Many thoughts ran through her head. How would she ever deal with Eugene and his infidelity? Even though, she'd grown to love Taylor, would she have moments where she despised her? When was God going to fix this whole thing? Did He even care?

She sniffled and roughly wiped her face.

"You know what, forget it all. Forget everything. God, I don't want to work it out and You know what," she looked up saying, "You might as well just keep *not* fixing it. Just forget it all."

She got out of the car and slammed the door. Angrily, she walked into the hotel and up to her room. She'd made her mind up that she wasn't going to pursuit Eugene, she didn't want to work anything out, and even more, she wasn't going to ask God to help with any of it.

***

Eugene sat on the floor, in Taylor's room, with his back up against the wall. Literally and figuratively. Taylor lay sleeping soundly in her crib. He thought about what his brother had said, a little over an hour ago, before he left.

Eugene, I can't stay all day with you, man. I have a life and I got stuff to do. Now, I know all this new to you, but you gotta find a way to deal with this. You better ask God to help you or somethin' cause, I can only do so much.

Before Julius left, he fed Taylor, bathed her, and put her to sleep. Only seconds after his leaving, Eugene hurried to his liquor cabinet, to retrieve a bottle of Crown Royal. As he took sips of the brown liquor, he stared at Taylor, through hazed eyes. He felt so defeated. He didn't have a clue about what to do with the baby. With *his* baby.

He sighed heavily and shook his head. Then, he sat his drink upon the window seal and lay down, in the cradle position. As he dozed off to sleep, overcome by his drunkenness, he slurred, only half-serious, "God, I guess you better help me."

***

Eugene lazily opened his eyes. As they came into focus, it took him a few seconds to remember where he was and why he was laying on the floor, staring at carpet. He stretched, rolling over unto his back. Then, he brought his wrist to his face, so he could look at his silver and gold trimmed, Breitling watch. It was 3:03 in the am. He'd been sleep for over three hours.

He stared out of the slits of the blinds, at the night sky. He sighed, thinking, *Good thing she's still sleeping. I guess I'll just deal with her however I can when she wakes up.*

Still feeling a little groggy, he rolled over unto his side. He was prepared to lay there a little longer, but as he glanced over towards the crib, it almost seemed like she wasn't in it. He couldn't really tell, so, he raised himself up a little.

Suddenly, his eyes grew wide and he jumped to his feet. Because he was still feeling the aftereffects of the alcohol, he stumbled a little, as he took three, long strides to reach the crib. He stared in the crib, clenching the rails.

Where is she, he thought.

She was gone.

He frantically threw around the blankets and stuffed animals on the bed, even though, it was evident she wasn't there. In a panic, he looked around the room. In the corners. In the closet. He stumbled backwards, barely able to stand. He pressed his fingers hard against his temples, still feeling a little lightheaded.

He took deep breaths to try to help himself think more clearly and calm down. His heart was pounding. Sweat beads began to form on his forehead. He could feel anxiety rising. He didn't understand why, but he was scared.

He ran out into the hallway. He looked at the top of the staircase. Although, there were three extra rooms downstairs, the last thing he wanted to think was that she'd somehow made it downstairs. He also noticed the gate was still intact, blocking the stairs. He honestly hadn't remembered locking it into place, but he was relieved to know it was there. His head spun as he looked around. There was his room, Taylor's room, the room he used for his office, another one that Savannah used to workout in, and a bathroom.

"God, help me," he said, as his breathing began to pick up.

All the doors were opened, so, he was trying to think of which room to go in first, hoping that that would be the right one the first time. He quickly ran to his office, thinking about all the dangerous office tools available to her. There weren't many hiding places there, so, he didn't have to search too much.

She wasn't there.

Next, he ran into Savannah's workout room, which was smaller. Still, thinking about all the things available that could harm her.

She wasn't there.

Next, he thought that she'd probably be in their room, since it was familiar to her. He ran in, calling out to her. He didn't know if she would have enough baby sense to respond but he hoped she did. He looked under the bed.

She wasn't there either.

Worry was beginning to get the best of him as he began to think the worst.

What if she's in the bathroom? She could have fallen headfirst into the toilet.

He called out to her.

"Taylor!"

He got up, intending on going to the bathroom. Suddenly, he heard Roxy bark. It came from their walk-in closet. His head jerked towards the door. He could see that the door was cracked open a little, but it was dark inside. He ran over to it and snatched it open. He flipped on the light switch and doubled over in relief.

There she sat, in the middle of the closet floor, with Roxy right next to her. She smiled, making gibberish when she saw him. She had a rattle in one hand, that she was using to playfully hit Roxy. In her other hand she held a small bottle of baby powder, that was all over her, most of Roxy, and a lot of the floor.

"Oh my God," he said, exhaustively, as he fell to his knees.

Weakly, he crawled to her. Whether he wanted to or not, tears began to fall from his eyes. Tears of joy, tears of fear, and tears of regret.

"I'm so sorry," he said.

He grabbed her and fell back against the wall, bringing her to his chest. He hugged her tightly.

"I'm so sorry," he said through tears.

"I'm so sorry I've been neglecting you and treating you like I have. I'm so sorry."

He kissed the top of her head and looked up saying, "Thank you, God. I'm so sorry. Forgive me, please. I'm so sorry."

After he managed to calm himself down, he held her out in front of him and said, "You don't ever have to worry about me not being there for you from now on. I promise. I am going to be the best dad I can be for you."

She smiled, and he hugged her again.

"I love you," he said.

Although, he didn't know how it would feel to say those words to her, but it warmed his heart when they left his mouth.

He chuckled, feeling pretty good about himself and again, said, "I love you," more confidently this time.

She laughed, completely oblivious to just how serious that short, but scary ordeal was. He looked over at Roxy. She lay there, looking concerned, it seemed. Eugene had concluded that Taylor had climbed out of her crib and Roxy watched over her while, her dad, who should have been there, was passed out from drinking at his own pity party.

"Thank you for watching her girl."

Roxy got up and made her way over to him.

He looked up again and said, "Thank You, for watching over them."

With every step Roxy took, she wagged her tail and powder constantly fell onto the floor. He laughed, looking at the mess Taylor had made.

"Look at you two," he said, laughing.

He shook his head at his little girl and said, "Come on. Let's get you cleaned up."

Eugene hadn't realized how much he loved Taylor. As a matter of fact, he didn't even know the ability to love her was in him. Perhaps, it had been hidden under resentment and shame and regret and guilt, and it could only be brought to the surface of his heart by the terrible feeling of fear. He didn't know that the thought or feeling of losing her, your own child, could be so overwhelming.

It made him think of one of the sermons he heard Pastor Larry preaching. It's funny that this was one of the times he was actually paying attention. He talked about how, the way we feel as parents, when we lose a child, to the world or when they are literally taken from us, is exactly how God feels about us. It saddens Him to lose one of His children and He will continue to pursue them, leaving the 99, just for that one.

That day, Eugene had a newfound respect for God. That day, Eugene had a newfound respect for what it meant to be a father. That day, Eugene moved Taylor's crib into his room, so she couldn't escape anymore.

Chapter 28

Neither Savannah nor Eugene had been to church since Eugene had returned home. For Savannah, there had been so much tension in the home, she didn't want to go to church and have to "put on front," like everything was peachy keen between them. For Eugene, he only ever went because he was going with his wife. Sure, at times, he heard what was being preached, but most times, it only fell on deaf ears. Now, ever since Monday, when he'd gone to see Pastor Larry, he was honestly trying to make an effort to do better and get to know God himself.

There were other reasons for their absence from church like, neither of them wanting anyone to know about the baby. Neither did either of them really want to show up separated. Savannah cared greatly about what people thought. People knew that Eugene was out of his coma and had returned home and she didn't want to deal with all the questions and, most of all, the stares and whispers.

She'd much rather have someone say whatever they had to say to her face, but she knew how most of the "Christians" attending her church were. Eugene almost went because he hardly cared so much about what people would think or say about Taylor. His main concern was showing up without his wife and honestly, he wasn't ready for any kind of nosey questions or curious stares either.

Over the week, Eugene had been making an effort to get closer to God. He'd also been taking Pastor Larry's advice, praying that God would help him with temptation. He knew he had to ask somebody who was bigger than him for help because it was tough being a married man, who was separated from his wife, and didn't know what the outcome of their relationship would be. Yet, he knew he loved his wife and he didn't want to do anything else that could push her further away. Every day, with the help of God, getting through the days seemed to get a little easier for him. Less painful.

Savannah, not so much. She'd been seriously going through the motions. Hating the doubts she was having towards God. Wondering if and when He would work on her behalf. Wondering if He even cared.

***

Eugene sat at the kitchen table, looking at a new client file that he'd gotten. Although, his colleagues asserted that he take as much time off as he needed, he insisted on working, for more reasons than they knew of. He looked up at Taylor, who was sitting in her walker, eating some snacks he'd given to her. Roxy lay next to her, as always. He smiled and then, he went back to looking over his file.

Only a few minutes had passed when he heard the doorbell chime. He looked up, concerned at who might have shown up unannounced, but eager as well, wondering if it could be Savannah.

He got up from his seat and walked quickly towards the door, but then, he slowed his paced thinking, *Why would it be Savannah? She has a key.*

He shook his head, disappointed at the thought of it not being Savannah. Then, he thought that maybe it was one of the cops that were posted outside of his house. Even though, Michael Espinoza was in jail, awaiting trial, along with some of the people working with him, the cops were told to continue their watch for just a little while longer. Just as a precautionary measure.

Eugene understood they had to do that, even though, he wasn't scared of who Michael Espinoza was or what threats he might make. He'd been threatened plenty of times and was not shaken by it at all. And now that he'd been getting to know God more, he was even more confident that nothing would happen to him.

When he reached the door, he peered through the peephole. He was able to see that there was a woman on the other side of the door, but he didn't know who she was.

He opened the door and said, "Hello. Can I help you with something?"

The mocha skinned woman, wearing red lipstick, flashed a big smile and sweetly said, "Well, I was hoping that there might be something I can help you with, Mr. Carmichael."

Eugene frowned a confused frown and asked, "I'm sorry, do, do I know you?"

"Oh," she said, as she flipped her long, black hair, which cascaded down her back, "My name is Cheryl. Cheryl Green. I attend the same church as you."

He thought to himself, *Surely, you didn't go today,* as he quickly glanced over the short, black, tight-fitting dress she had on. It had a very low, v-neck cut in the front and she wore some black, open-toe, high heels with it.

"Okay," Eugene said, as he folded his arms across his chest, waiting for her to state her business.

"So, yeah, um," she paused, being as sincere as possible as she said, "I had heard about all the stuff that's been going with you and your wife. And I'm not trying to get all up in your business, but I was just wondering what could have caused such a nice couple to separate."

She paused, as if waiting for Eugene to fill her in on what was going on in his marriage. When he didn't say anything, she said, "Anyway, I'm so sorry."

She made a sad face, pouting her lips, like one would do a child who'd hurt themselves.

I bet you are sorry, he thought, wondering how she knew anything about what they were going through. He believed in his heart Pastor Larry had nothing to do with this, but it did make him think about his mean secretary who'd heard a lot of their conversation the day he showed up to see Pastor Larry. He figured, she must have been the talebearer.

He nodded, "Okay," still waiting for her to state her business.

"Yeah, so, um, I," she bent over and took her time to rummage through a black, tote bag.

Eugene noticed the way her dress rose up her thighs and the way her bosom almost fell from inside her dress. He cleared his throat, quickly diverting his eyes towards the clear, blue sky.

"Brought you," she continued, finally pulling out a pie and presenting it to him, "An apple pie."

She flipped her hair and smiled.

He chuckled a little. He couldn't believe this was happening right now. No doubt, he's had plenty of women try to throw themselves at him, but he perceived that, he must see it differently now that he has been getting closer to God. He concluded that his spiritual eyes must have been more enlightened to what's really going on.

He smacked his teeth and said, "Um, you know what, I just ate so, I'm not even hungry."

He noticed she wasn't looking at him anymore. Her curious gaze seemed to be looking past him. He turned to look behind him and saw, Taylor, who'd obviously made her way over towards the door, in her walker.

He cleared his throat and pulled the door closed saying, "Like I said, thanks, but I'm not hungry."

Cheryl frowned a little.

"Um, is she yours? Because she looks just like you, but I don't remember you two having any..."

Her voice trailed off as it seemed she was starting to connect some of the dots. What dots, Eugene didn't know and neither did he care.

"Is that all," he quickly asked, a little frustrated that she'd even come over.

She looked at him and smiled.

"Hey, whatever happened with that is your business but, um," she moved a little closer saying, "Maybe, you could just keep it for later. I'm sure you'll like it. Everybody just *loves* my apple pie."

She subtly licked her lips, in a seductive fashion.

"Yeah, uh, I don't even like apple pie."

Forgive me, Lord, he thought.

He lied. He loved apple pie. Give him some vanilla ice cream and some apple pie and he was good.

She moved closer and this time, her intentions were more obvious as she looked at him and asked, seductively, "Oh, well, what do you like?"

Eugene had honestly been trying to let her down easy, but, *Dang,* he thought. *These demons are persistent.* He couldn't deny that she was indeed, a fine, looking woman, but he didn't want her. Not just because of Savannah and his new relationship with God, although, those were the main reasons. He was always turned off by a woman who tried so hard to throw themselves at a man.

He thought about one of the scriptures Pastor Larry had given him to meditate on. It was James 4:7.

Resist the devil, and he will flee from you.

"Look," he quickly said, "Thank you, but no thank you."

Obviously offended by the rejection, she said, "Hmph, she must really have you whipped."

He chuckled, thinking, Okay. *I see what's going on. Now, she's trying to target my manhood. But, it's all good.*

He looked at her and said, "You know what, she does. Now, goodbye."

He began to close the door but stopped, saying, "And please, don't ever show up to my house again."

She looked at him in disbelief as he closed the door in her face. He looked at Taylor, who was sitting idle in her walker. Then, he thanked God that he wasn't drunk with alcohol and self-pity. He'd already played that game and it cost him a lot more than he ever thought.

He smiled at Taylor, then, stooped down to her level, saying, "Hey, you ever had apple pie with vanilla ice cream?"

She smiled and bounced up and down in her walker.

"I knew you hadn't."

He thought for a second, then, said, "At 9 months, it's time for you to start eating some real, good food."

He chuckled, and she bounced around again, babbling at him.

"Let's go get some. It's gonna blow your little, virgin taste buds away."

Chapter 29

"Daaaang," Julius said, "She was bold for real, for real."

Eugene nodded his head, "Yeah. She really was."

Julius and Eugene sat around in the sunroom at Eugene's house. They'd just finished playing a one on one game of basketball, in the back yard. Taylor sat in her play pin, on the patio, playing with her toys and watching baby TV shows. Eugene had just finished telling Julius about his surprise visit from the lady from church.

"You talked to Savannah yet?"

Eugene used his red, sleeveless shirt to wipe sweat away from his brow and shook his head, "No. Not since we saw each other in Pastor Larry's office. I've texted her a few times, but she obviously has nothing to say to me."

Julius nodded. "Could you read her attitude or body language in any way? You know, as far as if she was ready to come back home?"

Eugene sighed heavily and answered, "Nope. I could tell she had an attitude. I could also tell she'd been crying."

He frowned a little, mad at himself, then, he smirked, adding, "But, she was always so good at hiding her real feelings. I know she loves me. I can see it in her eyes."

Julius nodded, slowly, wondering how long Savannah was going to act as if she didn't want to be home. Julius had come to know Savannah too well. He knew how much she loved his brother. He also knew that, when a woman loves as hard as she does, an act of infidelity as such, can be a tough pill to swallow. Therefore, he completely understood her hesitation. And the more he thought about it, he didn't know whether she would come back or not.

"I can say this," Eugene said, cutting into Julius' thoughts, "I don't know what Savannah's plans are, but I have hope."

He looked at his brother and smiled, nodding assuredly.

Then, he looked toward the sun that was now beginning to set and said, "I have hope because, ever since I've been giving God a try, I mean, really getting to know Him, for myself. Not just piggy backing off of my wife and the God she knows, but really putting in an effort to spend time with Him, I've noticed some changes. I mean, at first, I couldn't even look at Taylor, hold her, hug her, or anything, but ever since I asked God to help me with that," he threw up his hands saying, "I can't stand not being around her."

He shook his head and laughed.

"Not to mention, Him giving me the strength to turn down that lady because," he turned to Julius, "I could have had her. She was too easy, bro."

They both chuckled as Julius said, "I hear ya, man. I don't know if I *would have* or *could have* done that."

They laughed as he continued, "I'm serious. I mean, Lord knows I'm tryin' to do right, but hey, I ain't married and I ain't that saved."

They both laughed.

"I don't know what being "that saved" means, but I ain't there yet."

They laughed again.

"I feel you, bro," Eugene said, still chuckling.

"But," he cleared his throat, "In all seriousness, man. Taylor…"

He looked at Taylor, as she sucked on her pacify, playing with her toys. He smiled adoringly at her.

"That's my baby. That's my little girl and I love her."

They both fell silent for a split second and then, Julius jokingly said, "Yo, shut up. You gone make me cry."

They both chuckled.

"I know right," Eugene said. "But see, my point is, I never thought I would get to *this* point. With that being said, I just have to try my best to trust that He'll send my wife back home. I mean, if He can do *this*," he pointed to Taylor and then, himself, "Anything is possible with Him. Right?"

Julius slowly nodded, "That's what the Word says and I can understand where you comin' from cause I been doin' some soul searching myself. I didn't mention this when I came over the last time to help with the baby because I didn't really know how things was gonna go but, you remember Tracy?"

Eugene thought for a second and then, said, "That's the one that you had your last kid with, right?"

"Yeah and, well, we been tryin' to work stuff out, you know? See where things can go."

"Okay," Eugene said, nodding in an approving way. "So, is it official? Are y'all together?"

Julius nodded, "I mean, pretty much."

Eugene laughed saying, "What that mean, Ju. Either y'all together or not, man."

Julius laughed and said, "Okay, yeah. We're together."

"Alright then, family man."

Julius rolled his eyes and smacked his teeth saying, "Here you go with the jokes."

"Naw," Eugene said, chuckling, "For real. I'm happy for you, bro. I really am."

Julius smirked, "Thank you."

Eugene looked towards the floor and said, "It's nice to see somebody's relationship working out."

Julius looked at his little brother. He could see the hurt on his face. He hated that he was going through this. It hurt him to see his brother hurting like this. Yet, he knew he had to go through it. It was his *own* decision that produced his *own* troubles.

"Gene," Julius said, as he placed a comforting hand on his shoulder, "I know I can't do much but, I'm here for you, bro. You pray for me and I pray for you and we can keep prayin' together. And in the meantime, and in between time," he smiled at his attempt to rhyme, as did Eugene, "Just keep trustin' God, like you said. I believe He gone work it out."

Eugene nodded, saying, "You right. Thanks, Ju."

They both exchanged a heart-felt, brotherly hug.

"Now," Julius said, as he pulled away from Eugene, "I know you can trust God to fix yo' marriage, but I don't know if you can trust Him to help you with this butt whoopin' I'm bout to give you, in this basketball game."

Eugene smacked his teeth and said, "Let's go!"

Chapter 30

Savannah sat alone, on one of the back pews, in the church. Sure enough, she was too ashamed and embarrassed by her current situation to attend church on Sunday morning, so, she figured she'd go to Wednesday night bible study. She knew that less people attended church on Wednesday nights. Yes, Savannah was struggling greatly to overcome this mountain set before her and her own feelings towards God, but she knew she needed Jesus in her life.

Pastor Larry was preaching about forgiveness. As Savannah listened to his sermon, she couldn't help but shake her head and chuckle. Pastor Larry didn't know she would be there that night and up until 30 minutes before bible study would start, she didn't know she was coming, but she knew that God knew she was coming. Which is why she was hearing this message right now and feeling so convicted by it.

"I understand," Pastor Larry said, as he stood in front of the podium, dressed casually in a dark purple, collar shirt, blue jeans, and some khaki, Dockers shoes, "That some things can be devastatingly hard to forgive. It may even take you a while to do so and sometimes people never come to forgive the other party involved, but the thing we need to remember, church, is that forgiveness sets us free."

He paused to wipe the sweat forming on his forehead, with a white hand towel.

"You may think that you're hurting the other person by not forgiving them, and sometimes the other person may have their regrets, but the person you're hurting most is yourself. In some cases," he chuckled, "The person you're mad at doesn't even know you're mad at them because they didn't even know they did anything to offend you in such a way."

Savannah looked at her phone which sat face up, beside her. She noticed that her blue, notification light was blinking. She knew that meant she had a text message. She grabbed her phone and unlocked the screen. She saw that there was a text from Eugene. It read:

I miss you. Can we please talk?

Her hand rested on the phone as she sat it down beside her. She watched Pastor Larry as he spoke, but she wasn't listening. Her mind was elsewhere. Thinking about Eugene. How much she missed him. How much she missed Taylor. She smiled at the thought of her.

She looked down at her phone again and then, she turned away from it. As she was doing so, she noticed a lady, who sat not far from her, staring at her. Savannah knew she'd caught the lady off guard by the way she jerked her head back towards the direction of Pastor Larry. She'd seen the lady around, but she didn't know her by name. She wrote it off as nothing.

She grabbed her phone and looked at the text message again. She knew Pastor Larry was right. Yes, she was definitely upset by what Eugene had done, but a big part of her wanted him to hurt. She wanted him to hurt by her leaving him and she believed he was. But while she was wanting him to hurt, she couldn't deny that she was hurting as well. Yet, she loved him, and she missed him. She missed them.

She responded to the text:

I miss you too. I'll come by in about an hour.

Within seconds, her phone vibrated. It was a message from Eugene containing three, happy faces. She smiled and lay the phone back down, feeling good about her decision.

After service, Savannah decided she'd go to the restroom to groom herself a little, before heading over to see Eugene. She pushed open the door to the ladies' restroom and went into one of the stalls. Immediately, after she closed the door to the stall, she heard the restroom door open. Then, she heard the sound of heels hitting against the floor. She figured it was just some other lady who had to relieve themselves.

Cheryl, stood in front of the long, wide, restroom mirror, running her fingers through her long, black hair. She took out her cellphone and set an alarm to sound in one minute. Then, she went into one of the stalls, just as Savannah was exiting hers. Savannah proceeded to the sink to wash her hands. As she finished, she heard a chime come from the lady's phone, who'd come into the restroom after her. Savannah assumed, like anyone probably would, that she was receiving a phone call.

As Savannah retrieved her red lipstick from her purse, she heard the lady say, "Heeey handsome."

Savannah smiled, slightly, as she put on her lipstick.

Cheryl giggled, flirtatiously, and said, "Well, what do I owe the pleasure of receiving a call from Mr. Eugene Carmichael?"

Cheryl giggled again.

Savannah froze in mid stroke of applying her lipstick. Curiosity, nervousness, and fear arose as her facial expression changed to that of worry.

"Did you like my apple pie," Cheryl asked.

There was a brief pause and then, she said, "I knew you would."

She giggled.

"How is that pretty baby doing? She know she look just like her handsome daddy."

There was another pause, as Savannah's eyes grew wider. Her stomach churned. She felt like she was going to be sick.

How could she know about Taylor If she hadn't been over there? I mean, sure, she could've seen the baby at church when she came with Tiffany and me, but how could she know she was Eugene's?

"So, when can I see you again?"

Pause.

"Oh, I saw the way you were looking at me," she giggled, then, she said "How about I give you a call later tonight?"

Pause.

"I'm looking forward to seeing you too," she said, seductively.

"Okay. Bye handsome," she said, right before ending her fake phone call.

Savannah had been stuck in a serious trance, but when she heard the lady unlocking the stall door, she continued to prep herself as if she hadn't been affected by anything. As hard as she tried, Savannah couldn't help cutting her eye at the lady in the mirror. She tried to be as inconspicuous as possible.

She noticed how she emerged from the stall, wearing a big smile on her face. As she strolled up to the counter, straightening out her tight, baby blue dress, which Savannah believed was a little too inappropriate for church, she realized she was the woman who'd been staring at her earlier.

To the natural eye, it seemed like Savannah was holding it together so well. The truth was, she was livid! She was hot all over. She didn't know what she might say or how she might act if she stayed in that church building any longer. She gathered her purse and began walking towards the door. Her legs shook slightly, with every step she took because she was so upset.

As Savannah walked pass her, Cheryl glanced over her left shoulder and asked, "Hey, have we ever met? Do I know you?"

Savannah looked at her, almost in disbelief. She started to say something ugly, but then, she caught herself. Savannah knew the lady recognized her. They may have never spoken to each other, but they'd seen each other in passing at church, and on many of those occasions, Eugene was right by Savannah's side. Savannah was not sure what game she was trying to play, but she was not in the mood to be a part of it.

With a slight smirk, Savannah said, "We both know you do."

Then, Savannah continued towards the door. When she exited, Cheryl rolled her eyes as a big smile spread across her face. Savannah walked fast through the church building, trying to avoid anyone who seemed like they wanted to chat. Once she exited the building, she picked up her pace, almost jogging through the lot to her car. She dug in her purse for her keys and hit the unlock button as she approached the car. As soon as she got in the car and closed the door, she broke down crying. She hit the steering wheel as she cried, almost uncontrollably.

"I feel so stupid," she yelled.

In her rage, she grabbed her cell phone and opened the text that Eugene had sent. She began typing, and at the same time, angrily reading aloud every word she typed.

"I-hate-you-you-stupid-piece-of..."

She stopped.

She screamed loudly, "Aaaaargh! Why am I allowing him to make me act like this? To stoop this low, to the point of cursing him out? I hate the power I gave him! I hate him!"

Forgiveness, she heard.

The word escaped her mouth in a breath of disbelief.

"For-forgiveness?"

"Does he really have the right to treat me the way he has, and I'm just supposed to bow down to him?"

She rapidly shook her head, not wanting to hear anything from God, any logic, nor any reasoning.

"I am *so* done."

She opened the text from Eugene and deleted what she'd previously typed. Then, she typed:

Never mind. I'm not coming. I'm never coming back.

Then, she immediately powered off her phone.

***

Eugene had been devastated when he received that out-of-the-blue text from Savannah. He wondered what could have happened so suddenly. He'd been so excited. He had instantly called his brother, who was more than happy to come get Taylor after learning that Savannah was coming over.

He'd ran around the house, tidying up the place. He even lit candles and took out an expensive bottle of 1959 Dom Perignon to chill. Afterwards, he had jumped in the shower to freshen up. It wasn't until he got out that he realized he'd gotten a text from Savannah.

Immediately, he called her twice, back to back, but both times it went straight to her voicemail. He gave up because he knew his calls and texts would be useless. For the remainder of the night, he lay in bed, embracing a pillow, until he fell asleep.

Chapter 31

Eugene, the best thing you can do is pray for your wife.

The words Pastor Larry said to Eugene, the following day after Savannah said she wasn't coming back, presented themselves every time he thought about how much he missed her. And every time they presented themselves, he did exactly that. He prayed for her, all the while, encouraging himself.

Over the next couple of days, Eugene engrossed himself in his work, Taylor, and spending time with God. He was happy that one of the most important relationships in his life had been mended. He figured, if God could change his heart towards his daughter, his hope was that God could somehow change Savannah's heart towards him.

He had even rededicated his life to Jesus. Although, like a lot of people, he was baptized as a child. But even with that, he questioned whether he was truly saved. Not that he ever did anything so bad, but he questioned it. He questioned it because, also, like a lot of people, he felt that his baptism wasn't something he took seriously because it was more his mother urging him to do it than him deciding to do it for himself. So, not only did he rededicated his life, he wanted to be baptized again. And that's exactly what he planned on doing.

"Hey my pretty, little lady. What are we gonna do on this lovely Saturday?"

Eugene smiled at a freshly, bathed Taylor. He'd rubbed her down with all the baby oils and lotions he had. Then, he dressed her in a cute, pink onesie, with matching booties. He watched her as she rolled over unto her stomach and position herself on all fours, preparing to crawl.

"Whoa, now, slow down," he said, picking her up.

"I can't have you falling off of the bed."

She smiled, speaking baby gibberish. He looked at her adoringly and smiled.

"I'm glad you're here with me," he said, softly.

"I love you."

She smiled.

He could feel his emotions beginning to arise as thoughts of Savannah began to creep his mind.

"Okay," he said quickly, "How about we watch movies all day and eat pizza and junk food? Well, I'll eat pizza and you can eat a little bit of junk food."

He carried her downstairs saying, "I remember that last time I gave you some chocolate ice cream," he shook his head, "Whew! I did not have fun changing those diapers."

Chapter 32

Saturday night, and here I am all cooped up in a hotel room while he's probably out having a good ole time.

Savannah jumped up from the unmade, King sized bed she'd been laying around in for the last three days. She looked herself over in front of a wall mirror. She stood there, barefoot, wearing an oversized T-shirt she once got from a trip to the Bahamas. She ran her fingers through her uncombed hair and sighed.

"Savannah, you could at least brush your teeth and comb your hair."

She scoffed and said, "This is ridiculous. There's no reason why I should be sitting in this room, bored, and looking crazy."

She rolled her eyes, saying, "I'm sure Eugene isn't just sitting around, even if he does have Taylor with him. It's obvious he knows how to get around that."

Maybe, Tina would want to go out with me.

She grabbed her phone from off of the bed and sent a message to Tina, asking her if she'd like to go out somewhere with her. Savannah didn't mind going out by herself, but it had been so long since she had, and she would have felt more comfortable with someone else there.

Afterwards, she stared at herself for a minute or two, finger combing her hair in different styles while posing a little in front of the mirror. She looked at the phone.

Tina probably has to work, she thought.

She looked at herself for a few more seconds, then, she abruptly went over to her suitcase and began to rummage through it for something to wear.

I know I have something nice to wear in here, she thought.

Suddenly, she heard a notification chime on her phone. She grabbed her phone from off the bed and looked at it, expecting to see a text from Tina, but instead, it was a text from Eugene. She sighed, staring off into the distance, wondering if she wanted to read his text right now.

For the most part, every time he sent a text, it would say, 'I love you' or 'I miss you.' Being that, she'd been in a negative mood, since they split, his words usually added more resentment to her mood. She decided to open the text, figuring, it would only help with her decision to go out.

Savannah, I know you're not talking to me right now, but I wanted to share this with you because this gave me even more hope about us. I was reading the bible and I came across this scripture in 1Corinthians 7:15. It says, "But if the unbeliever wants a divorce, let it take place." Now, I know that you have grounds to divorce me because I did commit adultery. My heart breaks every time I think about how much I hurt you, but I don't want to leave. I do not want a divorce.

Although, you know, I was baptized as a child and received Jesus as my Lord and Savior, I have recently rededicated my life to Jesus. I am a believer. And this believer does not want a divorce. So, Savannah, with that being said, as Romans 4:17 says, I will "call things that are not, as though they were," and I'm going to believe that my wife is going to come back home. I love you. Goodnight.

Savannah looked over the message a few times. She had to admit, she wasn't expecting that.

She pondered on the message, thinking, *He's probably just trying to use the word of God to get to me.* She scoffs, *Ain't no way he changed that darn fast. I mean, he was just eating someone else's apple pie.*

She looked at the text again, trying to decide on whether she should respond or not. She wanted to believe what he was saying. She wanted to believe that everything would turn out the way she secretly hoped it would. Seconds later, she tossed the phone on the bed, allowing fear, pride, doubt, and a hint of stubbornness to decide for her.

***

Savannah stepped into a lowly lit lounge called The Red Room. She'd never been there before, but in her passing by, in search of somewhere to go, she decided to stop there because it seemed to have a reasonable number of cars in the lot. She figured it must be a nice place to go.

After thinking twice about paying the $10 to get in, she entered, as loud music, a mix of noises, smells of alcohol and smoke, filled her senses. She decided to play it safe by choosing to wear black, silk dress pants, and a black, wrap-around, silk shirt, with black heels. But now, she felt completely overdressed.

She could tell right away that she was in a place that was not tailored for older people. Although, she did spot some old heads, there seemed to be more people in their twenties to, early to mid-thirties in attendance. She started to turn around and leave but after thinking about the $10 she'd paid to get in, she decided against it. She figured, it wouldn't hurt to sit at the bar and have a glass of wine, then, go home.

She made her way over to the bar, which sat in the center of the lounge. She was cut off by one of the waitresses that hurried past her, carrying a drink in one hand and a small basket of fries in the other. That's when she noticed all the waitresses wore black bras, with black boy shorts, covered only by fishnet body suits and some kind of black heels.

She quickly thought about Eugene. She felt bad for him and any man who was trying to live life the right way. There was so much temptation out there available to everyone. So many handsome and beautiful people. So many who used their looks to feed on their lusts and weaknesses, as well as, others. She sat on a red bar stool, thinking, *It has to be so hard for some people to be faithful.*

Then, she thought about what she was thinking. She didn't want to make an excuse for him or any other man. Any person, for that matter.

I don't care how a man or woman dresses or looks, they need to have more self-control or stay away from the temptations that will feed into their lusts.

As she sat there, she thought to herself.

What are you doing here Savannah? She shook her head. Has it really come to this? Coming out to a lounge...bar...club, just because of what you're going through? Just because you want Eugene to hurt. How is he hurting, anyway? He doesn't even know you're at the lounge, she sighed, *the club. Stop trying to dress it up, Savannah. It's a club. Maybe, I should let him know I'm at the club. See how he responds to that.*

She shook her head, causing herself to snap out of all the thoughts going through her mind.

I should go, she though.

As she started to get up from the bar stool, the waiter, a younger, shirtless, African-American man, who wore a black bow-tie with black slacks said, "Excuse me, ma'am."

Ma'am, Savannah thought. *Even, he knows I'm old.*

"The guy at the end of the bar offered to buy you a drink. What can I get you?"

Savannah looked in the direction the bartender had gestured to and spotted a man, staring at her. There were, at least, eight people in between them, and thanks to the dim lighting, she could hardly make out how he looked. She could see that he was flashing a smile at her, though. She almost decided to decline, but thought, *Why not? That could be my free drink for the night.*

Flattered, Savannah said, "Umm, white wine, please."

The handsome waiter smiled and winked at her, acknowledging her order.

After a few minutes, Savannah was handed a glass of White Wine. She held it up and mouthed the words, "Thank you," to the guy at the end of the bar. In return, he held his drink up and nodded his head, smiling.

Savannah took her time sipping on the wine. She enjoyed drinking wine, occasionally, and usually, she'd only do it with Eugene or at least, only at home. This was mainly because she knew the affect that wine could have on her.

As soon as she finished her drink, she slid the bartender a five-dollar bill and yelled, "Thank you."

He nodded, saying, "Thank you," as he slid the money into his pocket.

Savannah cautiously got up from her seat, unsure if the wine had taken any effect on her or not. To her surprise, she felt fine. After taking only about five steps, trying her best to maneuver through the crowd, she felt someone grab her arm and say, "Leaving so soon?"

Savannah swung around, wondering who in the world could be grabbing her. She stared into the face of a handsome, dark chocolate man, with fine, shoulder-length dreadlocks. When he smiled, her slight frown of confusion, faded away. She knew he was the guy who'd bought her the drink.

She sighed, "Oh, yeah, I was going to head out."

He leaned in closer, so that he could speak into her ear, saying, "But I was hoping you'd let me buy you another drink."

Wow, he smells good, she thought.

"Um," she said, hesitating, "I don't know, it's getting kind of late and I have to drive."

"Oh, I can take you home," he said, smiling slyly.

I bet you can, she thought.

"Come on," he said, "Please? Just one drink and a little conversation."

What would it hurt?

She held up a finger saying, "One drink."

He, in turn, held up one finger. Then, he grabbed her hand and led the way to a lounging area, further away from the loud music.

Savannah grinned, thinking, *He likes to take charge. I like that.*

Quickly, her grin faded as she thought, *Stop it. Why did you even think that?*

She pulled her hand away from his as she followed him to a suede, red loveseat. She sat down and then, he sat next to her, making sure he was close but not too close for comfort. In all honesty, it was still a little too close for Savannah, so she scooted over just a little. Afterwards, he ordered them both drinks.

He looked at her and smiled, which made her smile.

"You have a beautiful smile, you know that," he said.

She smirked a little and said, "How fitting of you to start with the compliments."

He looked confused saying, "What are you talking about?"

She looked at him sideways.

"Come on, now," she said. "Isn't this how it always starts? A person meets someone and starts whispering sweet nothings in their ear, and they buy them a couple of drinks to get them drunk, all because the other person thinks that they just might get lucky that night."

He placed his hand over his heart, looking as if he were offended and said, "Wait, are you trying to get me drunk just so you can get lucky tonight?"

Even if she didn't want to, that got a laugh out of her.

"What's your name beautiful?"

"Savannah. And you?"

"Trent."

He held out his hand to shake hers and said, "It's very nice to meet you, Savannah."

She shook his hand and said, "It's nice to meet you too, Trent."

Almost two hours, and two drinks later, three for Trent, they'd talked briefly about their childhood and even some of their favorite things. Like, what their favorite colors were. Their favorite foods. Their hobbies. Their likes and dislikes.

Savannah was sort of mad at herself for allowing that conversation to happen. She always called those types of questions, getting-to-know-you-questions. Before she started dating Eugene, she stopped any guy whom she didn't find interesting, as soon as he started probing questions as such, making it clear that she was not interested in getting to know them.

Now, as Savannah stared at Trent, while he talked about something that was going in one ear and out the other, she studied his face. His dark, smooth skin. His nice, full lips. His perfect teeth. His clean shaven, facial attire which wore just enough stubble. It seemed that he had suddenly become very attractive to her. Not that he wasn't already easy on the eyes, but she knew that the lust of her flesh was getting the best of her. And, of course, the buzz she was feeling didn't help either.

It's been a while, she thought. *Help me, Lord.*

"You ok," he asked.

"Huh," she snapped out of it. "Yeah. I'm-I'm okay."

"I was asking if you wanted to get outta here?"

He shrugged saying, "We could get something to eat or, you know, anything you wanna do."

She smirked saying, "Anything *I* wanna do, huh?"

"I mean, you're the one that's been trying to get me drunk. I'm just saying."

"Whatever," Savannah said, laughing.

They exchanged looks and smiled. Savannah looked at the glass she was holding. The white wine was almost gone.

She sighed, thinking, *Eugene did it. What's so wrong with me doing it? I bet it'll hurt him really bad if I did go home with this guy. He didn't think about my feelings. And besides...*

The rambling that was going on in her mind was interrupted by Trent. He was gently rubbing her back.

"Let's go," he said, in a seductive whisper.

He got up and grabbed her by the hand, gently pulling her towards him. She stood up and followed his lead out of the door, leading to the parking lot. As she walked, following close behind him, his hand still cupped around hers, her thought process went into overdrive.

God, I don't know what I'm doing. Why am I about to go home with this guy? Am I about to go home with this guy? Is it just lust? Revenge? Loneliness? A little of all of that mixed together? What is it?

She shook her head as they walked through the lot. She assumed they were heading towards his car.

This is not right, she thought.

"Trent," she pulled away from his grip, saying, "This is not right. I'm sorry."

"What's wrong," he calmly asked.

"I'm so sorry. I-I wasn't trying to lead you on I just...I'm just going through some things right now and..."

She looked at him and sighed, saying, "I'm married. I mean, my husband and I are separated, but I'm still married, and you are so handsome and such a nice guy, but I just can't...I-I can't..."

He shrugged and said, "It's okay. I'm married too."

Savannah shook her head, confused.

"Oh, well," she said, taken aback "Are you...are you two separated or something?"

Unfazed, he shook his head, "No."

Still, even more confused, Savannah stepped back asking, "Um, where were you going to take me tonight?"

"Back to my house," he casually said. "She's out of town right now."

Savannah stared at him. She couldn't believe that he was being so nonchalant about it all. So unaffected by his marriage and what it was supposed to mean. As if he was sensing she was bothered by his outlook on his marriage, he said, "I mean, she don't care. She probably cheat too."

Savannah's mouth dropped open as she scoffed.

She threw her hands up and said, "Okay."

She slowly backed away.

"Okay. You know what? Thank you. Thank you for the drinks, but most of all, thank you for being so honest about who you are. You just woke me up and showed me that I definitely don't need to be out here."

Savannah turned away from him and headed towards her car.

"Savannah, come on."

Without looking back, she held up her hand and waved goodbye.

***

Sure, Savannah had dodged, what could have been a big regret for her, but she was still fuming. Not only was she mad at herself for almost making a really bad decision, she was mad at Eugene, all over again, and she was even more upset at how watered down the meaning of marriage had become to a lot of people. As she sat in her car, angry tears fell from her eyes.

"I'm so mad right now," she said aloud.

"How could I let myself get so caught up with this guy? This, married guy? And to make matters worse, I was going to go home with him? You're still married, Savannah! Are you crazy!?"

She quickly bounced her knee up and down, getting herself worked up even more, as more tears of hurt and anger fell from her eyes. She hastily rummaged through her purse, in search of some tissues. She didn't find any, so she quickly opened the glove compartment, knowing there would at least be some napkins in there.

She turned on the inside lights and felt around in the glove compartment, her eyes blurred by tears. She was irritated by her lack of finding what she needed and by the fact that the glove compartment was so cramped with papers and whatever else she'd thrown in it. She pulled most of its contents out and lay them on the passenger's seat, as some fell on the floor.

She successfully spotted a napkin from a fast food restaurant. She used it to wipe her face and nose.

Then, she began to angrily, stuff the contents from the glove compartment back in it, and at the same time, mumble and complain about the guy she'd just encountered, Eugene, her life, and any and everything else that came to mind.

"I can't believe that guy. And Eugene. He probably thinks the same darn way. My life is such a mess. What am I going to do from here? You know what," she said, briefly looking up, addressing God, "I don't even want to know. I guess I'll just do whatever I want and see how things turn out. It doesn't even matter anymore," she said, as she continued to shove things into the glove compartment, "I'm just so fed up. With all this crap. I can't take it any..."

She paused when she spotted a white envelope, with some writing on it. It caught her attention because, although, it was white, it had a red heart drawn on it, with the words: To: Mrs. Savannah Carmichael, From: Tiffany Poole.

Savannah frowned as she picked up the envelope, wondering what it was and what was in it. Tiffany never mentioned anything about it so, it really piqued her curiosity. She sniffled as she opened the sealed envelope. She pulled out three, white, folded papers. It was a letter. When Savannah unfolded it, she noticed, in the top, left corner, the date. It had been dated two days before her passing.

"Wow," Savannah whispered.

She was almost afraid to read the letter, wondering what words Tiffany may have been speaking from the grave. She took a deep breath and reclined her seat, preparing herself for whatever was to come. She let her eyes fall upon the words.

Hi. Mrs. Savannah. I honestly didnt know how to start this letter cause I really didnt know what to say but I knew I had to say something. And I never wrote a letter to nobody before so I'm just gonna write it how I write it and say what I have to say. I know I had already told you that I was sorry about the part I played in your husband cheatin on you but I wanted you to know that I really really am so so sorry. You have been so nice to me and Taylor. You helped me so much. More than anybody in my whole life and the more I got to know you the worse I felt about doin what I did. I wish I could of took it back.

I know it takes two and he played his part in the whole situation but honestly Mrs. Savannah I felt like a lot of it was on me to cause I really played off of his emotions. Thats what I knew and thats what I was

good at. I wanted money. That is all my motive ever was. I knew if I could get money from the men who wanted to give it to me I could easily get it from your husband. Why? Cause I could tell he was at his weakest and I played off of that. I told him what he wanted to hear. If I didn't know how to do nothing else I knew how to play a man to get what I wanted.

All he did was talk about you. Vannah. How much he missed you and how you wont talk to him and how it had been so long since you had made love to him. I had took him to one of the back rooms so we could have some privacy and talk. At least thats what I told him anyway. I knew alcohol played a big part in everythang so I made sure I gave him a lot of drinks to keep him liquored up. That was one of the mottos for us girls working there. And plus I didnt feel to bad for him cause I felt like he should not have come in the strip club anyway if he was so in love.

He was telling me how he had never cheated on you before. A lot of men say that but for some reason I didnt think he was lyin. He looked like he was bout to cry. I just stayed feeding his ego. I stayed comforting him. I was being the woman that he needed at that time. That is another motto us girls live by. One thing I can say is that I had never met nobody like him. The men that came in there didnt even mention they wife most of the time even though they had the wedding ring on. I could tell he really love you. He told me about how you was dapressed cause you had lost the baby you was pregnant with and I was really hoping he would shut up talkin cause I started feelin sorry for him.

But then I had to remember what was more important. Me. Me and what I wanted and how I had to survive. Honestly it wasnt like I really needed the money at the time but whats better than havin money? Havin more money. And when I found out I was pregnant and I knew for a fact the baby was his I really felt like that was a pay day. Specially after I found out who he was. And just so you know he did use a condom but sometimes the girls poked holes in them to use on people like celebrities or people that got a lot of money. So I figured it could of been one that had holes in it.

Mrs. Savannah all the stuff I said in this letter is stuff I really could not say to your face. That's why I hid it in your car. I hope you find it when you supposed to. I was to scared. But since I been around you and we been goin to church I can tell things been changin with me. I dont even like Jace no more. He get on my nerves so bad. I felt like if I wrote this letter I would feel better because I could really get some things off my chest. I don't know. I really cant explain it but I just want to say that I know Eugene did what he did but I played a big part in it to. I hate to think that a happy home might get broke up cause of me. Cause of Taylor. Thank you for being so nice to her. If anything ever happen to me I would want her to have a mama like you.

Please forgive me Mrs. Savannah and please forgive your husband. I know he love you. And I can honestly say that I love you too.

Goodbye

She looked at the letter, then, she hugged it to her chest.

"Thank you, Tiffany. So much. Thank you."

Savannah sat up as she lifted the back of her seat. Her eyes met the black and red, brick building. She watched as, even after midnight, the line was just as packed as it was over three hours ago.

She shook her head and said, "What the heck were you doing coming here, Savannah?"

She replied, "I don't know," answering herself.

She laughed.

She was surprised at how much that tickled her. Perhaps, it was because she knew she had no business being there in the first place. Regardless of what choices Eugene had made, or anyone else, she had to think about her own salvation. After a brief, hearty, much needed laugh, she lay the letter on the passenger side seat and started the car. Afterwards, she drove back to the hotel, determined that this would be the last night she stayed there.

Chapter 33

"Pastor Larry, I want to get baptized. And Taylor too. Can we please do it today?"

Pastor Larry stared at Eugene as he stood in the doorway of his office, holding Taylor. He'd just ended a telephone call, right before Eugene barged into the office.

Pastor Larry casually sat down in his chair, saying, "Um, Brother Eugene, you gone have to learn how to knock one of these days."

Flushed, Eugene laughed a little and apologized, "Pastor Larry, I'm so sorry and I promise it won't happen again I just, I just want to be baptized, you know? I've been baptized before, but it wasn't my decision. And I'm almost certain Taylor has never been but," he paused to take a breath, trying to gather his thoughts, "I want to do this for God. For me too but, for God. I want Him to know I'm serious. He said we have to do it right."

Pastor Larry knew he was referring to the scripture in Matthew 3:13-15, when John the Baptiste questioned his worthiness to baptize Jesus and Jesus replied that "...It is proper for us to do this to fulfill all righteousness," therefore, doing the will of God.

He looked at Pastor Larry, seriousness written all over his face, and asked, "Right?"

Pastor Larry looked at the man who held his daughter. He could see the passion and excitement all over him. He always admired how fast those babies in the Lord grew when they were just "baby Christians." He admired his passion.

He smiled warmly and said, "Well, God must have been looking out for you because we have baptism Sunday every 4th Sunday and it's the 4th Sunday. I mean, we usually have you sign up for it beforehand, but hey, if Jesus can just show up without John the Baptiste knowing when He was coming, why can't you?"

Eugene chuckled a little, nodding his head. He liked the way Pastor Larry jokingly made a reference to the same scripture he was referring too.

"Okay then," Eugene said, smiling.

Pastor Larry got up from his seat and made his way over to Eugene. He laid his hand on his shoulder and said, "Come on, my brother. Let's get you two prepared to be baptized."

***

Savannah sat on one of the back pews, in the far, left corner. It always seemed darker in the back of the church. That's what she was aiming for on this sunny, cloudless, Sunday morning. Why? Because the bags under her eyes were a serious case. To her, anyway.

If she could have worn sunglasses, she would have. Instead, she used as much concealer as she could without looking like a crazy woman who didn't know how to apply makeup, and most importantly, when to stop. She played it safe by wearing a plain but cute, black, thin, sweater-like dress, with sleeves that cropped around her elbows. She had on a pair of black heels and her hair lay stylishly, flat against her head. She also added her favorite red lipstick to her lips, to add color.

She had planned on calling Eugene soon after church to see if he wanted to get together to talk. She knew he would, but she seemed a little nervous, anxious even, about meeting with him. She wasn't sure why. She stood up with the rest of the congregation as the choir director queued the music. Savannah clapped along as the choir, made up of about 15 men and women, sang an upbeat gospel song.

Perhaps, I'm just excited to see him. Or maybe, I just don't want him to see me with these suitcases under my eyes.

She sighed, *I'll just call him tomorrow after I get a good night's rest. Yeah. Maybe, I'll do that.*

She continued to clap along with everyone and suddenly, she let her hands fall to her side. She shook her head, more at herself.

Savannah, girl, get over yourself. You know that man will be happy to see you no matter how you look.

She chuckled and said, "Help me, Lord. I'm a mess. I'll call him soon after church."

Then, she continued to enjoy the song selection. After the choir finished singing all that they had prepared for that Sunday, everyone continued to stand as Pastor Larry made his way on the stage. He stood behind the podium, draped in a purple robe, and led the congregation in prayer. Afterwards, everyone took their seats.

"Good morning to all of you, beautiful people."

"Good morning," most of the congregation said in unison.

"You know, every day is a lovely day, when the Lord sees fit to allow you to see another day. But it makes it an even better one, when you decide to proclaim your decision to follow Jesus Christ, publicly."

"Amen," someone said.

"That's right," another one said.

"And that's what we'll be witnessing today. So, let's get started!"

Applause and praise erupted from some of the members in the congregation. The gold curtains were drawn back, revealing the baptism tub. Brother Henry, a brown-skinned, bald, short man, stood in the water, ready to receive those participating, as Pastor Larry stood off to the side, ready to introduce them.

"Okay," Pastor Larry began, looking at a sheet of paper he was holding, "First, we have someone who has been a member of our church for 3 months now. Although, she was baptized as a child, she informed me that now, at the age of 81, she would like to be baptized again. Everybody, please help me welcome, Mrs. Patti Lyons."

The congregation clapped as Patti Lyons, an elderly, grey-haired, Caucasian woman, cautiously made her way down the steps, wading into the water.

"How you doin' today, Mrs. Lyons," Pastor Larry asked.

He put the microphone up to her mouth and she replied, in a sweet, high-pitched voice, "Oh, I'm doin' pretty good, Pastor. The Lord saw fit for me to wake up this mornin' and so, it's a good day."

"Amen, amen," Pastor Larry said. "Do you have any family joining you today for this special occasion?"

"Yes sir. I have my daughter here, with her husband, and my three grandchildren."

"Let's have the family stand, please and give them a hand."

On the other side of the church, a nice-looking family of five, briefly stood up, as everyone clapped for them.

"Well, Mrs. Lyons, I'm not gonna hold you up any longer. Let's get started."

Brother Henry said, "Mrs. Patti Lyons, do you declare that you have accepted Jesus Christ as your personal Lord and Savior?"

"Yes sir, I declare," she replied.

A few people laughed, including Pastor Larry and Savannah, because it was simply, a sweet moment.

"Please, pinch your nose for me."

Mrs. Lyons pinched her nose shut.

"Mrs. Patti Lyons, I now baptize you in the name of the Father, the Son, and the Holy Spirit."

Then, he briefly submerged her into the water. After she came up, she shouted, "Hallelujah!"

Everyone clapped as Brother Henry helped her out of the water.

Pastor Larry said, "Praise the Lord. Okay y'all, we gone keep it movin'."

One by one, Pastor Larry introduced four more people wanting to be baptized. Through it all, people clapped and applauded, as family members of the participants, were acknowledged. Rejoicing, along with others, as their loved ones were submerged and brought forth out of the water. Savannah sat back and smiled, enjoying the celebration with everyone else.

"Alright y'all, we got one more. Well, two more, but they're doin' this thing together. You'll see why in a few seconds. This wasn't a planned baptism, well, at least, not on paper, but this person rushed into my office this morning telling me how bad he wanted him and his daughter to be baptized and of course, I was not going to turn him away. I mean, really, what would Jesus do?"

There were a few chuckles from the congregation, but most were wondering who this mystery person was, including Savannah.

"Without further ado, everyone please help me welcome, Mr. Eugene Carmichael and his daughter, Taylor Carmichael."

While some exploded with applause, as Eugene emerged from behind the curtain, holding Taylor, others clapped, slowly, wearing looks of confusion. As for Savannah, the only thing that had moved was her jaw, as her mouth fell open from surprise. Those sitting by her, who knew who she was, couldn't conceal their confused and curious stares.

She groaned, thinking, *This would happen the day I show up.*

After the crowd had calmed its applause, Savannah sat still, staring straight ahead, avoiding the looks she knew she was receiving.

"Brother Eugene," Pastor Larry said, smiling, "I'm glad to have you two here."

Eugene smiled saying, "We're glad to be here."

Pastor Larry turned to address the audience, saying, "Of course, this is very unconventional. Baptizing two people together, but I see nothing wrong with this."

"Amen," someone shouted.

Pastor Larry started to turn back to Eugene, then, he hesitated. He had been asking for everyone's family who was in attendance to stand and he knew it would only be proper to do it for Eugene, as well. He intended on doing so, but first, he had the urge to ask, "Before we get started, Eugene," he turned back towards him, "Is there anything you want to say?"

Eugene hadn't planned on saying anything, but as soon as Pastor Larry put the microphone up to his mouth, words, nervously, began to break free. Savannah listened, attentively.

"I," Eugene began, laughing nervously.

He cleared his throat and continued, "As Pastor Larry said, this wasn't a planned baptism. I mean, this wasn't even a planned speech for that matter but," he sighed, "God has a lot of plans we don't know about, right?"

"Amen," some from the congregation said.

"Um," he said, unsure what to say next.

He looked at Taylor, much of the reason for a lot of the stuff that had gone on over the last few months and smiled.

He cleared his throat again and said, "You know, it's hard to say that something was a mistake, when what comes out of it is such a blessing."

He lowered his head for a brief moment and then, looked up saying, "Yes, this is my daughter, Taylor. And for a lot of you who have known me and my wife, Savannah, since we've been coming to this church, you know that we don't have kids. Some of you may even know about the problems we've experienced with trying to have kids."

He sighed heavily and said, "I say that to say, I'm sure a lot of you have already figured out that Savannah did not have Taylor. Yes, I made a temporary decision, by being unfaithful to my wife, and it has cost me greatly. My wife and I are separated right now, and I don't know if she's coming back."

He paused, gathering his thoughts, obviously hurt.

His voice cracked as he said, "I wish she would."

Savannah looked towards the floor, still, not wanting to make eye contact with anyone, especially now.

Eugene cleared his throat again and said, "Yet, I believe that God will work that out."

He looked at Taylor and smiled, saying, "As for Taylor."

He stopped for a moment, almost unable to speak because he'd become so overwhelmed with emotion.

"As for Taylor, this little girl, who came from one of the worst decisions that I could have ever made, has been such a blessing to me. I mean, at first, I couldn't touch her. Hold her. I couldn't even speak to her."

He shook his head and held up a finger.

"But, God…"

"Amen," some shouted.

"God, along with much counsel from Pastor Larry, helped me see her in a different light. I began to see myself differently. God gave me the strength to deal with the choice I had made, and He helped me get through it. And now, I can honestly say that I love her."

He shook his head saying, "I wish my wife were here because, what she doesn't know is that, her actions towards Taylor, allowing her to live in our home and caring for her the way she did, it spoke volumes to me. Savannah displayed so much of what Jesus would have done in this situation. So much love. So much grace. And I love her dearly for that. And, even though, she's not here, I want to publicly ask for forgiveness from God, from her, and from all of you because you're my family too."

Eugene laughed a little at how emotional he'd gotten and said, "I'm sorry y'all, I just..."

"Come on, let it out brother," Pastor Larry said.

"I just," he continued, getting chocked up, "I just want my family back."

He bit his lower lip, trying his best to keep his emotions in check, which had already begun to overtake him. He laughed and said, "Pastor Larry, let's get this baptism started. I'm starting to cry too much."

People laughed, including Pastor Larry as Eugene wiped away the tears that had fallen from his eyes.

"That's alright, Brother," Pastor Larry said, who'd had a hard time not shedding a tear or two himself.

"You know," Pastor Larry began, "It's a beautiful thing when you're able to confess your sins so openly and ask for forgiveness with a whole heart. Beautiful thing."

Pastor Larry turned to him and said, "I forgive you, Brother, and I'm sure the church and God feel the same way. But, I'm ready to get this thing started."

He turned towards the congregation and shouted, "Are y'all ready to see these two baptized?"

"Yeeees," the congregation shouted.

Pastor Larry turned to Brother Henry, but then, he stopped himself and said, "I almost forgot to ask, if there is anyone here, that is a part of this beautiful family, if you will, could you please stand?"

People looked around to see if there was anyone standing. Those around Savannah, who knew she was in attendance, looked at her.

Savannah was looking down. She was beginning to get hot, from embarrassment, anxiousness, fear, and shame. She wanted to stand up, but another part of her didn't. Sadly, she still cared about what others thought about her. About the whole situation. Yes, she had decided she would talk to Eugene afterwards, but she didn't want to be put on the spot like this. No. Not like this.

Eugene didn't know whether Savannah would be in attendance or not. Even if she was there, at this moment, he didn't know if she would even stand up in support of them. He hoped she would, but he was so full of wanting to please God and trust in Him, he decided to leave his marriage and the sadness it brought him in His hands.

"Well," Pastor Larry said, "That's alright. Hey, you have a big family right here in this church. How about we all stand to celebrate this wonderful moment with the both of them."

Everybody in the church stood up. Everybody, except Savannah.

Lord, help me, she thought. *What am I afraid of? What is it? I do love him.*

"Alright," Brother Henry said, "Eugene, have you accepted Jesus Christ as your personal Lord and Savior?"

"Yes, sir, I have," he replied, nodding.

If Eugene can get up there and confess all of that to the people here, before God, why am I being so fearful? So nervous? I do love him.

"And Taylor," brother Henry said, smiling, "Have you accepted Jesus Christ as your personal Lord and Savior?"

Pastor Larry put the microphone up to Taylor's mouth and she made a cute, cooing noise. Aws came from the crowd.

"That sounds like a *yes* to me," Pastor Larry said.

Laughter erupted from the crowd. It was such a sweet moment. Even Savannah giggled, as her eyes became teary-eyed.

Help me, Lord. Help me. You said that you did not give me a spirit of fear, but a spirit of power, and of love, and of a sound mind. I do love him. I love Taylor too. I do. I really do. That's my family. Yes. That's my family. My family.

"Wait! I'm here!"

Savannah jumped up from her seat as if it were on fire. She hastily made her way towards the front of the church shouting, "I'm here. I'm here. That's my family."

She looked at Eugene, as she stood in front of the stage, with tears in her eyes and said, "That's my family."

Eugene's eyes welled up with tears as he said, within his heart, *Thank You, Father God, for answering my prayers*.

It was almost too hard for anyone there to keep their emotions intact, including Pastor Larry, as he said, "Brother Henry, take it away."

Brother Henry swallowed hard, overcome with his own emotions and said, "I now baptize you two, in the name of the Father, the Son, and the Holy Spirit."

Eugene covered Taylor's mouth and nose as Brother Henry quickly lay them both back in the water. As soon as Eugene emerged, he shouted, "Thank you, Father God! Thank you!"

After wiping away the excess water from Taylor's face, he looked at Savannah and smiled, mouthing the words, "I love you."

With tears streaming from her eyes she yelled, "I love you, too."

Then, Eugene, dripping wet, carefully hurried out of the water, making his way to where Savannah was.

When he reached her, he looked at her lovingly, and passionately said, "I missed you."

With a big smile and tears streaming down her face, she nodded and whispered, "I even missed you while I was sleeping."

Chapter 34

"Look at her face," Eugene said, laughing.

Savannah giggled as she looked at Taylor. They sat on a bench, in the back yard, while Taylor sat close by, in her high chair. She was digging into some of her leftover birthday cake, where most of it ended up on her face. Roxy, of course, faithfully sat close by, wearing a birthday hat.

Julius and his wife, Tracy, stayed after to help clean up all the evidence of there being a birthday party, where about 10 toddlers and a magician was present. Savannah and Julius, who were beat, decided they'd sit around and enjoy the sunset on this nice, Wednesday evening.

"Hey, my baby. Hey, my pretty little girl," Savannah sweetly said to her.

Eugene sternly looked at Taylor and said, "You know you get your looks from your daddy, right?"

Savannah laughed and playfully hit him saying, "Hush boy."

"Come on," Eugene said, "Let's get you cleaned up."

He wiped her face and hands with some wet napkins and gently gathered her from the high chair.

Then, he sat her on his legs, holding her out in front of him.

"Now, you listen to your daddy, Taylor."

Savannah smiled. She loved to witness the way he tended to her. She loved how much of a great father he was.

"This is some of the most valuable information you will get from me. If a man likes you and you're not sure about him, ask him if he calls those white undershirts men wear, Wife Beaters or Muscle Shirts."

Savannah burst out laughing.

"You so silly," she said.

"I'm serious," Eugene said to Savannah, smiling. "She can do it in a casual way."

He turned his attention back to Taylor and said, "Just pull up a picture on your phone and say, "Hey, what kind of shirt is this?" If he says Wife Beater, and then he's smiling when he says it, go the other way."

Savannah laughed and said, "You got that right."

She looked at Taylor and said, "Say, bye boo boo."

They laughed.

They continued to enjoy that day they shared together, as their hope for the future, love for their family, and the love that God had so graciously showed them, continued to bring about nothing but good fruit.

Epilogue

Two court cases within less than two weeks apart from each other and Eugene and Savannah attended them both. The first, the sentencing for Michael Espinoza. After the evidence that Eugene had hidden was turned over to his colleagues, they worked tirelessly to make sure Michael Espinoza would never see the light of day again. He was given two life sentences for the crimes he'd committed and all those involved received their time as well.

Although, Eugene had received some threatening phone calls and a couple of letters from someone claiming revenge for what happened to Michael Espinoza, after a few weeks and much praying and believing, the threats stopped. Eugene refused to live a life of fear and chose not to worry about what anyone could try to do to him.

The second case the one that mattered most to Eugene and Savannah, was the case against Jace, for the murder of Tiffany. Although, the case had been handled by another firm, being that Eugene had ties to the mother, the prosecutor, an old friend, made sure that Tiffany would get justice. He came down hard on Jace, who had been found four months later, hiding out at some lady's house.

After some testimonies from people who'd been eye witnesses to Jace's violence, and a testimony from the young lady that had driven Tiffany to the motel that evening, he'd been found guilty. Although, the counsel sought the highest sentence that could be given for manslaughter, he only received 25 years to life, with the possibility of parole.

For Savannah and Eugene, it was a bittersweet moment. Yes, justice had been served, but like any family who lost a loved one, they always felt like it wasn't enough. All in all, they knew they had to eventually, forgive him, move on with their lives, and allow God to deal with his heart, as they dealt with their own.

The End

Things She Never Expected

Jaketa A. McClure

Reading Group Questions and Topics for Discussion

*1.*When Tiffany 1st showed up at the hospital, Savannah gave her some money. Savannah did not have to do that. Why do you believe she did? Would you have done the same? Why or why not?

*2.*Do you believe it was beneficial, for all the parties involved, that Eugene was in a coma? Why or why not?

*3.*Men like Jace come in all forms, shapes, and sizes. Why do you believe some women settle for men like Jace?

*4.*Savannah, full of resentment, went to a club, where she met a man named Trent. Before she decided against it, did you believe that Savannah would go home with him? Why or why not? Why do you believe she didn't?

*5.*Tiffany wrote a very heartfelt letter to Savannah. Was the letter an important piece in Savannah's decision to go back to her husband? Why or why not? Do you believe Savannah would have eventually gone back to Eugene without the letter? Why or why not?

*6.*As the saying goes, "It takes two to Tango." Do you believe Tiffany blamed herself too much in the letter she wrote to Savannah? Why or why not?

7. Was the information about Michael Espinoza enough, or do you believe his character should have played a bigger role in the story itself? Why?

8. Regarding Savannah and everything that happened, what were the things she never expected?

About the Author

Jaketa A. McClure is also the author of the young adult, fiction novel *Rodeo*. Originally, born and raised in Atlanta, Georgia, she now lives in Arkansas, with her three kids. Feel free to reach out to Jaketa at GIGPublishing.com, as well as, on Facebook or Instagram.